Black Jesus and Other Stories

D1245725

Black Jesus and Other Stories

by

Cyril Dabydeen

TSAR
Toronto
Oxford
1996

The publishers acknowledge generous assistance
from the Canada Council and the Ontario Arts Council.

Cover art by Aries Cheung

Canadian Cataloguing in Publication Data

Dabydeen, Cyril, 1945-
   Black Jesus and other stories

ISBN 0-920661-57-2

I. Title.

PS8557.A25B52 1996   C813'.54   C96-932074-4
PR9199.3.D32B52 1996

Printed in Canada

TSAR Publications
P. O. Box 6996, Station A
Toronto, Ontario M5W 1X7
Canada

CONTENTS

Birth

Ma said to take the cow inside the barn, and Dave, my brother, looked surlily at her. Dave was like that sometimes, and I knew he preferred being with the pigs.

Ma hollered because she was now angry. "Go on, Dave—go on!" At times she seemed like the cow herself, bawling; and it was the way the animal mooed loudly in the morning just before the sun was up that seemed to be getting to her. Ma fretted night and day. This began when my father left us, some time ago. The cow, it was the only one we had; and all of us wanted to take good care of it, especially since it would soon give birth.

Dave started squealing like a pig in protest, and I listened to the sounds he made, genuine caterwauling they seemed.

Ma hollered again for Dave to bring the cow inside, her face twisting like a corkscrew. Right then I decided to go and help Dave, though I wasn't supposed to, but I didn't like seeing Ma like this.

I pulled and dragged the cow to the barn at the back of the house among the acacia and black sage, and I said to her quietly: "Ho, now, girl, you'll soon have a calf. Be still. You're making everyone nervous. And maybe you're nervous too."

I was looking forward to the calf being born, same as Ma and the rest. The cow's large eyes, so immobile, almost as if they weren't eyes at all. The eyes began making me nervous. But I didn't tell anyone this.

Now the cow only wanted to holler, as if the calf inside her was starting to take the life out of her, which Dave somehow knew because he was squealing again, more loudly. Maybe this was why he didn't want to go close to the animal. Uncle Harry was right when he said something was the matter with Dave. But Ma had replied curtly to him, "Nothing's the matter with Dave." Uncle Harry knew when not to cross Ma. But I could tell from his eyes, the way they narrowed, that Uncle Harry believed something was the matter with Dave. My brother, you see, was just two years younger than me, and he'd sometimes be by himself and talk to no one but the pigs. Maybe he sensed things; that was what Ma once said, her lips twisting, as if she was thinking something else, something far away.

Dave, I knew, would look sternly at her right in the eyes; then he'd tell her things, and all you had to do was listen to him, carefully. He always seemed to know what was on your mind, just like that. Sometimes he sulked. Now I figured he was going against Ma herself; he didn't want to be close to the cow.

Ma shook her head as she came alongside me. She muttered, "Your Pa shoulda be here with us; he really left us a long time ago." She kept repeating this for no reason at all, a wistful look in her eyes. Then she looked at the cow and shook her head again, adding, "If he'd been here, Dave wouldn't be behavin' like this. It started happening just after he left, you see." She didn't sound bitter; it was just something that had to be said maybe, her words heavy, lingering in my mind.

What did Ma really mean by "it," as if Dave had some kind of mental illness?

She added, "He needs a father 'round here."

Ma kept talking more or less to herself, and I began thinking less about what she said. Uncle Harry was with us anyway, and sometimes he'd laugh, really laugh. He'd sit around late in the afternoon and tell us stories about when he was young, and then things about my father, which I liked hearing. I imagined Pa when he too was young. I'd find out things about Pa which no one ever mentioned before. Again Uncle Harry laughed; he seemed to be laughing louder with each story he told about my father. Maybe Pa was a little crazy himself, I figured; I too laughed. Not Dave, though. Once he said straight to Uncle Harry, "I don't believe you." His eyes burned, they had fire in them.

"You don't?" Uncle Harry stopped laughing.

"No," said Dave, looking away, as if he was some place else.

"It's true," Uncle Harry said. Then he continued laughing.

Now I wasn't laughing any more. And Uncle Harry kept looking at

Dave, thinking about him in a quiet way; maybe thinking that no matter how much he laughed, it wouldn't make a difference with Dave.

Dave was only eleven, but he looked older. The only time he seemed his age was when he talked to the pigs. He'd be talking to the pigs for hours, as if they understood every word he said. Sometimes I went close by, to listen in, wondering if he was really retarded; I'd heard this whispered, though I didn't know what the word *retarded* meant.

Ma said to me, "You shouldn't be watchin' Dave like that. He's your brother."

She always had a soft spot for him. So did I, come to think of it: which was why I didn't mind helping him from time to time with his chores, looking after the other animals.

Then I stopped eavesdropping on him, yet I imagined him talking to the pigs like they were people. Another time Dave kept smiling all by himself, still talking to the pigs, maybe remembering something or the other.

That night in our room, Dave said to me, "See, I been telling them stories. And they tell me things in turn."

"Who, Dave?"

"You know who." He smiled.

I remained quiet, thinking hard again about Pa.

Then he added, "I know you've been watching me. You can't fool me. Ma don't like what you're doing either." His face grew stiff, as if a strange illness was overtaking him.

I pretended to laugh, because I didn't want him to know I was afraid of him now. But I was. That entire night I remained awake, thinking. Once or twice I wanted to wake him up to ask him about Pa, if he knew where Pa was. And though his eyes were closed, Dave was still awake, thinking all the time. I began, "Where is—" then stopped, and waited, as I listened to him breathe hard. After about half an hour I asked aloud, "Where's Pa, Dave?"

He opened his eyes at once.

Thinking harder he seemed, then: "I don't know." Just as I figured he'd say. He closed his eyes again, pretending to be asleep.

"How come you don't know? You're always thinkin' about him, you can't fool me." I went up close to him in the darkness.

He squirmed, pulling the blanket to his face, eyes. Then he played at snoring, falling into a deep sleep, as I continued looking at him.

When I returned to my bed, I kept thinking about Ma and Pa as I'd never done before: what they were like when they were living together; and I began thinking too what Pa might be doing right now, wherever he was. But this was hard to keep up. Maybe Dave was doing the same, I figured, he couldn't fool me. Deep as his snoring was he was thinking about Pa more than ever.

Ma knocked on the door, feeling instinctively that we were somehow awake. "You still up?" she asked, as I pretended to be fast asleep.

Dave quickly got up and opened the door for her. Then he hopped back into bed.

"You okay?" she asked, moving closer to me.

"Yes," I muttered, turning over on the bed, away from her.

Ma whispered, "See, the cow's goin' to give birth in the morning. Have some good thoughts in your head."

"What for?" I turned again, irritated now. But I was also watching her in the dark. Dave, no doubt, again had his eyes tightly closed.

"Uncle Harry says the cow's not in good shape. She's a sick girl, he says. That's why she's hollerin' like that. She's not eating too," she said.

I thought about this, figuring Dave was now wide awake.

Ma looked distressed as she sat on the bed next to me. I could tell she really wanted another calf to start a herd, small as it'd be. If all went well, she wouldn't fret as much. Opening my eyes, I told Ma I would pray. She tiptoed out of the room.

For a while I remained awake, thinking, listening to her footsteps, then to the sounds the cow was making outside. The cow was moaning hard, and maybe it'd soon die, the calf inside her also. Suddenly I began praying, though I'd never really prayed before.

But the cow continued to moan loudly. When it began raining and lightning flashed everywhere across the window, I still heard it moaning. And very soon she'd die—I knew, as I turned in the bed once more and started to pray again, though the words didn't come easily. Now Ma was in the narrow hallway walking about, unable to sleep.

I sensed Dave was awake; I heard him turn once or twice. He didn't snore now, and I imagined his eyes opening, closing, as if he was in some

4

kind of a turmoil, just like Ma.

Ma opened the front door, going out in the rain; going to the barn, to see if the cow was really okay. And Ma sometimes talked to the cow, the way Dave talked to the pigs. She'd be doing this now, as I once more prayed, with the thunder rolling, lightning flashing. And the rain was coming down harder, the drops pounding on the roof. I imagined Ma outside being wet all over, and the cow too being wet and still moaning louder. For a long while I kept thinking about this, until I fell asleep.

The next morning, I saw Ma's eyes looking very red. She had bags under them, she seemed really tired. She woke up late, as I did too.

Then I already knew, because Dave was the first to tell us: he'd gotten up earlier than usual and found out that the cow had given birth to a calf. Loudly he cried this out to everyone.

"When?" asked Ma, shaking her head.

Dave nodded, as if he didn't want to say more.

"Is she okay?" asked Ma, rubbing her eyes fully awake and looking alarmed as she listened to Dave's high-pitched voice.

Dave kept looking at her, not saying anything. Mute, he seemed.

"You sure?" Ma pressed, then looked at me and seemed to become more fully awake.

Neither Dave nor I answered. But no sooner I ran to the barn where the cow was, to see for myself, Ma close on my heels.

The cow was frothing at the mouth, its eyes canting, swirling, as if it was going to die at any moment. Ma looked really distressed now. Then she looked at the calf beside the cow, how frail, pink it was, and beautiful too.

Ma smiled. Then she moaned, looking at the cow, her eyes fixed on it.

Dave standing next to me suddenly started to breathe hard. But he said nothing. Then he started trying to say something. Maybe he was muttering to himself, only, his mind working, heart pounding.

Uncle Harry came, and he looked grave. "It's a healthy calf," he muttered, rubbing its brownish grey coat and feeling the bones along its legs and shoulder, then looking at its eyes.

The cow watched helplessly, letting out a soft moan.

Uncle Harry continued rubbing the calf, looking at its tongue, pulling at its small mouth. Then he once more gave his full attention to the cow.

He shook his head after a while and said, "It's not going to live much longer."

Ma looked really worried. "You sure?"

Uncle Harry nodded.

I kept looking at the frothing cow and feeling really sad. And what was it like to die, to not exist anymore? I glanced at Dave, thinking of Pa . . . and maybe Dave, as before, knew exactly what was going through my mind.

He shook his head, intense as he seemed.

Now the calf was hungry as it lunged to suck at the cow's udder, pulling, then jabbing at it with its forehead.

Uncle Harry tried pulling the calf away, but it would rebound to the udder. Finally he managed to hold on firmly to the calf, keeping it still. He asked me to feed it, saying the cow needed all her strength. The cow needed to be left alone, also; there was no need for the calf to take her life away.

Before I could make a move, Ma ran to get a bottle, filling it with milk from the kitchen. She forced a nipple onto it, and plied it into the calf's pink mouth. At first the calf refused and hollered and squealed, not unlike a pig.

Dave laughed—surprising us.

The calf began to get used to the plastic nipple, the small mouth sucking hungrily, as if it was meant to do this all its life. How hungry it actually was I almost felt it now, the milk going down my own throat almost. I swallowed hard.

I turned my attention to the cow, which was frothing more and more. It was breathing slowly too, her dark eyes rolling mournfully as it looked at the calf still hungrily sucking at the nipple. Then the cow looked at Ma.

Uncle Harry shook his head again. "It won't last another night," he muttered.

Ma moaned loudly.

Dave hurried off to feed the pigs, the six we had altogether. We always seemed to have six pigs only; and Dave liked hearing them squeal. There was nothing he liked doing better. And the pigs came after him when he squealed, especially the piglets, chasing after him in a way as if after their mother. Dave laughed loudly; and at such times he was happiest, I could tell.

When I listened in on him again, I overheard him saying to the pigs, "Yeah, she's not goin' to die. Wait an see, they're wrong. That cow, she belongs wid us. She's one of the family; she's not goin' to die!"

I wanted to ask Dave if he was sure about this, so I could run back and tell Ma.

I didn't.

I merely listened to Dave, watching him for a while longer, how he behaved with the piglets. Then I went back to look at the cow—to watch it alone. Ma or me or Uncle Harry would keep watch like this; and all the time the cow moaned, then hollered. Ma was even more distressed now, but in her eyes I saw a glimmer of hope when she came near to me.

Ma again looked at the calf sucking at the plastic nipple at the bottle, seeming really glad to be alive.

Dave came too now, laughing, as if he couldn't stop himself.

Uncle Harry watched him and chuckled, all because of Dave's manner—just as I expected. Then Dave, as I knew he'd do, drifted back to the pigs to continue playing with them.

Ma watched him going away and muttered under her breath that Dave was like that since Pa had left us.

Uncle Harry remained silent.

I felt like telling them what I'd overheard Dave say to the pigs: about the cow not dying. But I decided against it—like a secret it'd be between Dave and me.

Uncle Harry had a funny look on his face, as he said to me, "Will it?"

"Will it what?"

He kept looking at me, expecting an answer.

"Will it die?"

I knew then I couldn't keep it from him any longer, secret or not. "That was what Dave said anyway," I murmured.

Ma looked confused, her face contorted in a mild paroxysm.

Dave was coming towards us again, whistling, looking really cheerful, as never before.

7

"Say, Dave," Uncle Harry called out, "come here!"

Reluctantly Dave came, fidgety, looking, anxious. Maybe he didn't like the tone in Uncle Harry's voice.

"So you t'ink the cow will live, eh?" It was as if Uncle Harry wished the cow was dead, wanting his prediction to come through.

"Yeah," Dave nodded, grinning, idiotic-looking.

Uncle Harry laughed, in a way laughing at Dave now.

Ma, she seemed more confused. She didn't know what to say or think.

Dave looked at me, and he figured I'd overheard him. And maybe I shouldn't have told Uncle Harry what I heard.

Uncle Harry turned to Ma, then once more to Dave with an odd expression on his wide mouth.

"How d'you know, eh?" Uncle Harry asked Dave pointedly, as if he was angry.

Dave shrugged.

"Come on, boy—tell me," Uncle Harry insisted, no longer grinning.

Ma looked from one to the other. Then she looked at the cow again, then at the calf which was still sucking away at the nipple, though the bottle was almost empty.

Dave didn't answer; he only looked determinedly at the cow. Then he started whistling again.

Uncle Harry didn't know what else to say. He shook his head glumly.

The next morning the cow was still alive. The frothing had stopped. The calf drew near the cow, and the cow's eyes brightened at once. Ma watched them all the time. So did I.

Dave came by, and he didn't whistle this time.

Uncle Harry didn't show up; maybe he figured the cow was already dead. Maybe—and what was the use.

Immediately I thought the cow wouldn't die. Ma thought so too, from the happy look on her face, the way she was smiling all the time. Dave slowly walked away from us.

A little later I heard the pigs squealing, louder than usual. A sound almost maddening. I ran to the pigs' trough, Ma close behind me, her heart thumping.

We were just in time to see Dave waving his arms about and angrily chasing the pigs away.

But the pigs were running helter-skelter, all around, some chasing after Dave, as if he was now their enemy. It was a sight to behold, so surprising it was. Then the pigs were running away from him, as if scared of him.

Ma hollered, "What you done to the pigs, Dave? What, eh?" She looked frightened, the same way Dave looked, horror written all over his face. And Dave cringed, lips pursed, tightening, and he started shaking all over.

Ma let out again, "Get after the pigs! Go on—get after them!"

I wasn't sure if Ma was hollering at me or Dave.

But Dave stood his ground, arms akimbo. He watched me take after the pigs, running here, there, in a circle, then in a straight line; next, turning around once more. And the pigs were really wild now, as if they weren't ours any longer.

Half an hour later, I returned.

Ma was alone. She said to me, "It's all because your Pa left us, see. It's been hard on him. It always been like that wid your brother."

I nodded, though I didn't fully understand her.

"Your Uncle Harry though, he should know better." She was scolding from the way her voice rose, her heart still thumping.

I looked around for Uncle Harry, and kept thinking of Pa—and what Ma just said. Yeah, one day I hoped to ask Uncle Harry why Pa had really left us. He ought to know, because he was Pa's brother.

I found myself looking for Dave right then, but he was nowhere in sight.

Mother of Us All

There was a shrillness about Auntie which echoed throughout our house; and sometimes she stamped her feet, raging, when my mother at the same time was given to silence. Such were their ways, which took my long growing up to find out. Auntie, scolding again, and there was none like her, as the children talked in hushed tones: we desperately wanted to be away from her, as far as possible. And we continued jeering, with defiant stirrings growing in me; and the older I grew the more I became aware of the difference between Auntie and my mother.

I looked at the others, noting the expressions on their faces, as their voices became shriller. And all the while my mother continued acting distant or far away. But Auntie's eyes widened with a determined will; and in hushed tones we talked about her, my own whirring, memory-words; and Auntie sensed I was on the verge of jeering once more. But she was preemptive, shouting at me, "I will get you, wait an' see!"

I watched her from a safe distance, laughing, despite a growing fear. Auntie reddened at the tips of her ears. She went to my mother to tell her about my ways. My mother's pulsating mind, thoughts resonant, mouth awry. "See that son o' yours," Auntie screeched. "See how he jeers." My mother kept silent, lips pulled in almost, dumbfounded. And then only vague mutterings escaped her lips as Auntie continued berating: "He needs a good scoldin', that boy!"

Me?

My father was gone for good now, I knew; he no longer lingered at doors, corners, looking back at me, us; and maybe he only whispered to me from afar, as I could still hear him.

"You should scold him too," Auntie repeated to my mother, about to start beating her breast again. "Scold him real good!"

My mother's lips twitched. Finally she said to Auntie, "Leave him alone." My mother's ways often baffled Auntie, as they looked at each other in silence. I sensed my mother's thumping heart; Auntie's pursed lips, mouth twisting.

I wasn't sure what made us behave the way we did. The harsh sun, with a scarce breeze blowing; or sometimes a strange memory whirling in odd places in our minds. And too I kept flipping through the pages of foreign magazines; I'd watch the pictures in them for hours on end, imagining people skiing down ice slopes from high hills, mountains. People in Canada almost everywhere were doing this it seemed; and how I longed to be like them, and to wear heavy, yet attractive clothes; and I'd dream about this, going down ice slopes at breakneck speed. In the night's darkness, I was also dressed in white, wearing thick wool on my already warm body.

My mother would come to me, muttering her silent words. Then, more clearly, "You must behave."

"Eh?"

"Behave. You must have respect for her, your Auntie."

"I have *respec'*."

She slowly walked away, into regions her own, as if into a leaden state. And she kept on talking, berating me, sometimes with pain in her eyes, even as I continued hurtling down ice-capped mountains—and I would never stop, the sun glinting at the tips of the ice everywhere as far as I could see. Faster I kept going. Then immediately dizzy I'd become. My mother didn't look back at me now, just when I wanted her to. I waved to her mechanically—and to no one at all.

Auntie passed by and said, "You wait an' see." Her eyes locked with mine for a moment. "Yes, wait an' see," she kept muttering and stamping her feet—her way. The others—nieces, nephews, the whole troupe of us—cried out in a chorus, "Wait an' see!" Mock admonishment, yet all our forlorn ways combined in this rhapsody.

Auntie scowled; and all the while my mother kept wondering, her eyelids making quick butterfly's wings; a eucalyptus creeping along a frayed window sill, as I watched her. Then, breathing in hard, I felt the sensation of the Atlantic trade winds tempering the heat. And everyone else breathed in hard—a strange accompaniment.

Auntie smiled, at last now her winning ways. My mother's face, cheeks dimpled; she remained motionless against another fresh breeze as she stood by the window, looking far out. It was her way of coping with the world, I figured, her understanding of the sun's rays, all that was outside; and smiling from time to time by herself, she was always alone.

When I went to the ice slopes again, coming down with dive-bomber speed, I continued thinking about her, her inevitable presence. Then smiling she was, praising me: "You've done it." Her almost mute exultation, song.

Now what was she imagining? And the nieces and nephews again jeered, shriller this time. I too laughed with them, while still thinking about my mother locked in her strange silence and anonymity.

Our family kept being like this day after day. Sun glinting on glass, and through it prisms of unfamiliar-familiar light. Earth's cracked signs and, oh, this rutted ground: always our real, unrelenting tropics. My imaginary temperate zone, intermittent, those foreign magazine images, lingering, everpresent.

Auntie grew mottled along her ears, forehead, as my mother forged on with an inside pain, throbbing at the centre of her being. We watched them, my brothers and I. Thunder rolled that night, lightning criss-crossing. A heavy downpour next, which seemed to go on for days, overwhelming all else. My mother opened and closed her eyes in quick succession, then her stranger ways of breathing; and that night I listened to the inevitable pitter-patter of further rain, then the pounding on galvanized zinc roof of our ramshackle house. I waited in vain for ice slopes to intermingle, reappear, as I kept listening all night long. Frogs croaking, crickets cheeping. A sonorous music everywhere, simultaneous requiem.

The next morning I meandered along the road on squelchy mud, my bare feet caked. Then slowly I reentered our house, with an odd but forlorn independence of spirit.

Auntie's admonishing voice, her tongue's rasp at once: "Go an' clean your feet!"

Silently, I obeyed. My mother looking at me—looking out too after the last squall of rain, mirroring the horizon in her eyes it seemed; her constant memory-ways. Who was she now? I didn't know, could never tell. She turned and again looked at the far trees, the horizon. Just then I remembered my father, in a mighty rage, sometimes seeming like a magician, appearing and disappearing: himself a trick.

Instinctively I waved to my mother from outside the house once more. But my mother didn't wave back; only signs of her mechanical breathing, and her words: "You must behave."

The others—children all—followed me, the eldest, as if I was a Pied Piper. They took orders one moment, but were recalcitrant another, with all their strange stirrings. And voices of dismay in me, in them, and further mock rage; and how they jeered louder, then virtually flung themselves through windows, doors, pounding their chests. Ah, they were real pests. *We all were!* And Auntie was once more alert, ready to intimidate: if she could. So it continued, day after day.

The older I grew, the more I watched Auntie: she at times starting to pound her own chest. Then the relationship between Auntie and my mother began taking a different form. Maybe Auntie now more than my mother wanted us to grow up well-behaved—such was her aspiration, her own pulsations of spirit at night.

But we couldn't be contained; we were still flying through doors, windows, at the snap of a finger. Caterwauling, creating havoc in the turmoil of longer days and nights—always in the tropics' own profligate seasonal change of weather. In the dead of night once more, and our fears took on a different turn, with palpable ghosts everywhere. Sounds unimaginable, all secret voices converging with images of fearsome reptiles, anacondas: they coiled and uncoiled under our beds, then in our dreams becoming nightmares. Lizards, too, their transparent limbs sprawled out in decipherable patterns against the sun-drenched windowpanes; next haunting us in crepuscular light; sometimes a mere foreshadowing in the shuttered light-and-dark.

Blankets quickly pulled over our faces, heads, that night. Our eyes, holes: our being awake in the deepening dark, as we nervously whispered out our fears. We felt compelled to it. And in the next room, all by herself, there was Auntie.

Again, *thud-thud-thud.*

The devil was coming alive now, drawing closer. In this way Auntie was still scolding, and she also wanted to frighten us more than ever. At once I imagined her a sorceress. Was she really?

Another methodic thudding sound, and just when I thought she had fallen asleep, it came again. *Who* . . . in the dead of night? The walls beating, like old wounds, so scared we were. We waited with bated breath, all of us. Was it really Auntie? Dreams now turning into solid nightmares. Veritable snakes coiling, uncoiling. We were defenceless, trapped by the indomitable dark. How we kept hoping the thudding would stop, memory-awakened as we were. *Auntie, where are you?*

We looked at each other, and quickly drew the blankets again over our heads. Breathing in harder, we listened to one another's fears. And I, the eldest, felt I had to be brave. The eerie dark was all around, overwhelming, and I felt I was alone with the unnatural sounds.

A faint, funereal howl from somewhere. Was Auntie still playing a trick on us, her ultimate revenge? Was she? Was this a witching hour? Ah, our ongoing frenzy, the ground-earth unleashing more fear, with all the nearby river's turgid memories, things lying deep under, unearthed.

"It's nothing," I whispered to the others cowering around me. "See . . . it's nothing."

They huddled closer, five or six, on the bed. My voice, weakening, "See, it's just her."

One laughed convulsively. Another started crying loudly.

"It's her . . . her," I tried consoling. "Ah . . . it's just her."

But none believed me. How could they in the swirling dark with sounds of backoos and ole higues: ancestral yet immediate spirits coming from the hovels of our minds. Hands stretched out; furrowed faces indeed in the spotted dark.

How they trembled next. We all did.

More quiet, sombre. And maybe Auntie knew she was having this effect on me—just as she always wanted. Just as she talked herself into doing, believing. And maybe she'd never have to scold again. *Never!* In the dead silence . . . she believed we were indeed scared out of our wits.

And where was my mother now? My father too? Thoughts humming, like oddly silent bees, in us.

We waited for the worst to happen. Then she came, my mother, watching us now in the trembling dark. She muttered a prayer, as we listened . . . and finally sleep seemed to save us from the further assault of our senses. Yet we twisted, turned interminably, all night long.

Morning's soft light, the heave of the dark away from us. A new day indeed; and Auntie's face was one of glee . . . as we watched her. *Who was she?* In the kitchen, she looked determinedly at me. All the while my mother stood stationary before the earthen fireside slowly putting in chopped wood in two-foot long pieces that were sometimes twisted, warped-looking. The fire smouldering, her eyes flickering, all her indescribable wounds. Her flesh tones, her inner self translucent. Blood of a kind, leaking out, crystal-shaped as I kept watching her from a far corner. The sun's shadow close by.

"So you're behaving now," Auntie said, with a face of remembrance of pain.

No answer.

My mother looked steadfastly into the fire, growing into a mild conflagration. Her own face's livid colours . . . as I concentrated harder.

Auntie continued with her gloating and irony. "So you're really behaving now," she repeated, as the glare enveloped the entire kitchen where we had gathered for our meal.

I nodded. But I was also silent, watchful.

Auntie looked smug, very pleased.

My mother turned around, then again kept looking into the fire, the hearth's own recesses; she waiting to hear more, of what happened last night, the uncoiling of the imagination's dark. Slowly she put another log into the fire, shoving it impatiently. The fire flared up at once . . . and just then I saw my father's face, appearing and disappearing. Now he was the one scowling. Last night . . . *he*? The thud-thud of almost ancient memory. My father somewhere, *close by!*

My mother poked the fire in a quiet frenzy. Tense, ribbed the veins on her hands. My stomach growled. One of my nephews let out a sound, and looked at me with a forced smile. All the others imitated him in a whisper, despite the fear of the previous night written on their faces.

Auntie close to me said, "You think you're still the same, eh?" She was scolding, but without her usual vehemence. The fire slowly dying, as she started handing out plates of flat bread, roti, the customary fare.

We ate quickly, while my mother and Auntie looked at us; and they also looked at each other.

My mother said to Auntie, "Is good that they eat."

Auntie mumbled a reply, her unique concurrence.

"They must be strong," my mother added.

Auntie, quickly, "They must behave too."

It was as if this was what she wanted to say all along, all night too, in the sombre dark; then, in the day's fire, eyes intermittently looking at us. And we were now fully before them, without memory-wounds, as we ate hungrily; and I kept looking at the others chewing quickly. They too looking at me, still recalling the night's dark images.

My mother suddenly smiled. Auntie also smiled.

At this particular moment: this special time of my life, I felt immediately grown up. I swallowed quickly, and began to feel nourished by their words, always in the fire's silence; words past and present; words' future. I swallowed again. The other nieces, nephews also swallowed quickly.

My mother turned once more to the fire, concentrating on its many shapes, forms.

Auntie, watching her, blinked.

In the hearth's darkness and light, the surfaces, brownness of skin: my own senses beating, as I looked, at them . . . and my mother's turnaround once more, with blood racing through her veins. Individual bones throbbing against her flesh, as I became aware of my own beating heart. And my mother and absent father were also in this frenzy, as I swallowed, a bunched knot in my throat . . . then I started coughing.

Auntie began laughing. She was, this moment, laughing harder, as I'd never heard before.

My mother, against the brightening fire, stood rigid, immobile, oddly expressionless; looking at me. And in her I saw my true self; I understood that deep inside me I nurtured a passion which I couldn't articulate; which lay hidden beneath my skin, yet kept coursing through my blood, in every crevice of my flesh, deep in my bone marrow. This, the self denying, undenying; this, my future beginning, belonging . . . to this end and place it would be . . . without snow-capped mountains. Here, with

Auntie's laughter still in the air, all her intermittent rage, also; and my mother's inner pain, against the sun. Snow glinting, at the tips of glaciers; and places yet to go to . . . and to remain, forever. Auntie's loud scolding no more; my mother's quiet, no more.

Going Places

He'd just come back from a far place, and now he seemed more determined to start "transforming" the village, the entire country, at this time of night; and it didn't matter if his wife, Goldie—my niece—was in the side room of our house at one o'clock in the morning about to give birth to their first child. Yet Verne kept admonishing his audience, mostly relatives keeping a "vigil"—waiting for the child to be born—as Grandmother and the other women, including the midwife Miss Davis, remained with Goldie in this hour of her "travail."

"The balance of forces in the world's changing," Verne cried, waving his hands, head bobbing. I kept an ear open for the soon-to-be-born infant's cry—a piercing scream as it'd be. Goldie would be really happy when this happened, I figured, she whom we used to call "Suck Lip" because of her strange habit of always curling in the lower lip and sucking or biting it. Now seventeen, Goldie was still like a child in some ways.

Verne looked at me, as we huddled in the living room. We were glued to him in a manner—the same Verne who'd travelled the world, the Party always sending him to one place or another . . . to Bulgaria, Hungary, Moscow, and more recently to Cuba—this much I knew. Each time Verne returned home, he resumed his long harangue, decrying capitalism and wanting something better. It would be his transforming zeal all over again.

In between listening to him, I kept imagining blood and water pouring from between Goldie's thighs as I'd heard happened when a woman was giving birth. The wall lamp flickering in a corner, and Verne's voice rose again: "In Russia, everyone can speak four or five languages." His mouth widened, like a strange parody. Again he looked directly at me.

I wanted to tell Verne he should be thinking about his wife, Goldie:

about her pain this moment in the side room; and didn't he care? Did it always have to be about *transformation,* about how good socialism was making the world become? Verne seemed to shrug me off; and maybe it was because I was still young, and I'd never travelled beyond our district. The wall lamp flickered against the men's faces as they listened intently to Verne, in contrast to the women in the side room busily attending to Goldie. I imagined the latter holding her hands, rubbing her legs, Grandmother chief among them; and I knew Grandmother didn't like how Verne often left Goldie "to travel the world."

Verne added, "See, we must do our best to make this country the first real socialist state in this hemisphere in South America." He thrust his head forward, ready to bludgeon us with his rhetoric.

"You sure about this, Verne?" I asked now, yawning a little and looking at the others—all workers—and wondering if they believed him.

A few also yawned, tired after their long day's work in the fields, and it being so late now.

Verne jutted his head forward, eyes brightening, as he trumpeted, "We've got to work together to bring about change. It is a moral duty for us to be united, you hear!"

"But . . . Verne . . . " I attempted, then stopped.

The others were still fascinated by him, their eyes lighting up at odd moments; and their hands, feet, gnarled from the effects of cutting sugar cane, kept twitching occasionally as a new thought aroused something in them. Verne perhaps was their only hope of escaping the life they lived, all their back-breaking work. And Verne sometimes extolled a good life: with his help before long they too would live a life of leisure and ease, and escape poverty once and for all. *We all would!*

But Goldie's face came back to me: all that she was going through in the side room; and I wanted it to be over. I waited anxiously to hear the newborn's piercing scream, the women still coaxing Goldie, asking her to bear her chafe, Grandmother more than anyone else. "It's a woman's lot," I'd heard her whisper. The oil lamp still flickered against the wall, shadows leapt, spurting odd shapes, silhouetting the men's faces. I followed the latter's gazes, their attention as they reverted to Verne again— who now laughed against the dwindling light.

And to me only, once more, Verne added: "You're young, but you'll see the difference one day."

The eye glasses rigid on his nose, thin as a rake as he was, Verne was perhaps thinking of eventually assuming leadership of the Party. No, he couldn't be a prime minister; a prime minister was made of sturdier, more dynamic stuff. But then I began having second thoughts the more he talked: it was suddenly possible with him—Goldie's husband—as Verne's voice rose.

I cocked an ear, tilting my head, still waiting for the newborn's cry. Muffled voices. The women's continuing anxiety, in faint cries, amidst Goldie's moans. The labour was taking a long time . . . something was going wrong.

Grandmother sighing, I figured. Verne sucking in air, having trouble breathing it seemed, as he wiped his glasses. Was he acting like this because of his own anticipation, excitement . . . his child actually being born? An older man sitting next to me with crooked, almost blackened front teeth, coughed. Maybe he too was thinking about Goldie's "travail", his face twisted, askew.

Verne started quoting . . . Marx, Lenin, then Jose Marti. He always had a new set of names, all authority figures, revolutionaries, at the tips of his fingers. "See, what I'm saying?" he cried, shaking his head. "The balance of forces in the world's changing all over South and Central America. Soon we're going to have our own working people's government. We will control our lives, our own destiny!" His hands struck out in the air, mouth twisted in strange excitement—so bent he was on his transformation zeal. He paused, allowing this to sink in: such was his rhetorical flourish.

Again I cocked an ear, waiting for the baby's cry. I also knew the men truly envied Verne because of his travels abroad—how we yearned to go to other places, to visit the neighbouring Caribbean islands: Trinidad, Jamaica, Barbados . . . *Cuba!* Sometimes I figured that if I stuck close enough to Verne, he'd one day take me with him to these places; though I'd also started giving up on this idea. Now, with his child soon to be born . . . it'd be a new phase perhaps.

I saw Grandmother coming out of the side room, the light dappling her face, patterning her cheeks, nose. Tired she seemed (Grandfather had died more than a year ago and she was left to take care of us all). The stillness of the village night descending on us. A dog howling funereally. Outside, the night blacker. A lopsided grin slowly came to Verne's mouth as Grandmother drew closer, and she seemed pained. One of the menfolk, as if unable to keep it in any longer, hissed: "How's she?" He meant Goldie.

Grandmother muttered, "It taking a long time. Goldie—she is—"

"Oh?" Verne asked in a chirpy way.

Grandmother didn't continue, she only winced. I winced too.

I expected Verne now to say he wanted to go into the room to see how Goldie was doing (though men were often forbidden to enter the delivery chamber, husbands or not); but at this moment I expected Verne to break this rule, he the world-traveller and revolutionary! The lopsided grin still on his face. Grandmother's stare was now like granite.

Then Verne slowly began to shrink away in the dim light, eyes smaller, his body about to disappear at any moment.

Grandmother added, "Goldie will be okay . . . maybe." Life and death summarized in her few words, laconic body language. Outside the dog howled louder. A dim moon hung low. The guava tree in the backyard rustled, presaging rain.

Verne muttered, "The baby . . . " his voice faint.

Grandmother sighed, her way.

I also sighed, then quietly started praying—asking God to assist Goldie, my favourite niece.

Verne cackled a strange laugh, as he said pointedly: "She needs to be in the hospital—same as they do in Russia. There all the babies are born in hospitals. And most of the doctors are women." It was as if he was now accusing Grandmother: it was her fault this wasn't so.

"Here," he added, raising his voice, "it's only superstition!"

Grandmother, again sighing, started walking back into the side room.

I rubbed my eyes, looking at Verne who raised his hands as he lamented, "My child will now be born in superstition. Goldie should be in a hospital."

As he went on, it was hard to follow him; the night grew longer.

One or two of the men in the living room nodded in half-sleep; but they'd wake up once they heard a sound coming from the side room. Verne's lips tightly pursed. I thought Goldie was now in more serious pain, the baby stuck between her thighs, unable to come out; and Grandmother and the other women were all urging Goldie to *push harder.*

Come on, Goldie, you must! Please. Your life and the baby's depend on it. Come on. *PUSH, PUSH!*

The image of the baby's head jammed, maybe; then the arms—left, then right. Blood pouring out brightly next. The women frantic, eyes bursting out of their sockets. Verne drew me back to him as he added, "We need to have a revolution here. Our people are being exploited by Europeans and Americans!"

Oh?

One of the men yawned. Another's eyes lit up, however; he immediately felt close to his bones the truth of what Verne was saying.

Verne added, as if before a large gathering: "The people here have always been slaves cutting sugar cane near two hundred years now!" He still kept being carried away.

Next he talked about going to Cuba again: there he'd seen changes, he swore. He mentioned Jose Marti's name again—the father of the Cuban nation, didn't we know? Then Che Guevara, Fidel Castro. I focused on the whites of his eyes—how they darted, like fireflies.

"It must end, it must!" he sang. "We must have solidarity with revolutionaries everywhere around the world!"

Should we?

Then I heard the baby's scream, a piercing yell frightening me. Yes, the newborn wanted everyone to be aware of its presence at once.

I got up quickly, almost delighted. Verne was still talking, the whites of his eyes darting. But the baby's cry was quickly overtaking all else.

The men shook hands, one or two laughing.

Verne stood up, being Fidel Castro now with a cigar in hand, and I immediately wanted to laugh.

"Yes . . . yes . . . " Verne added, teeth locked together, then free again. "The workers . . . "

Grandmother came out from the side room, face bright. She was telling us all was well. "The baby's fine," she emphasized.

But how was Goldie?

Grandmother's expression slowly changed. She looked at Verne, as if she wanted him to be aware of what she was about to say.

Verne looked at her too, somewhat anxious; he didn't seem as confident as before. There had been complications, no? Was Goldie's life in danger? I couldn't contain my own anxiety. I moved closer to Grandmother.

She appeared to wait for Verne—for *him* to ask about Goldie. But he was taking a long time, the words not coming out. The baby still bawling; and the men kept on smiling because of the new arrival in the world. Then they too sensed the tension, between Verne and Grandmother.

I prayed that nothing was seriously wrong with Goldie. And I didn't want Grandmother to keep us in suspense much longer.

Verne asked, with a squeak: "She . . . okay?"

The baby kept crying loudly: and maybe it was a boy. When a newborn cried so loudly it was always a boy; a boy's lungs were deeper, the cries stronger, so I'd heard.

Grandmother nodded, as if she knew what I was thinking. Her eyelids knitting a dozen flutters, winks. Her tiredness maybe. Then she looked at Verne, and suddenly she wanted to tell him that he belonged at home: with Goldie, especially now since the child was born. He shouldn't be going far away all the time, travelling because the Party kept wanting him to transform our country—to transform the world!

Verne dithered, nervous. Grandmother was making him react like this. And was he thinking she was only illiterate—she whom I had never seen read or write before? The baby's cry suddenly stopped.

Grandmother muttered, "Goldie's okay. But . . . the baby nearly *killed* her!"

"It did?" Verne asked, almost stupidly.

The other women started slowly coming out of the room, some looking exhausted. The midwife Miss Davis, face black like charcoal and flushed, came out last. Slowly Miss Davis went to the window. The early morning light was starting to stream in through the chinks, crevices. She blinked . . . was it already morning? The sun couldn't be out already, I thought, it being about four o' clock now; unless it was a full moon . . . as I again thought about Goldie, the way she and I used to play together as children, and her constantly sucking her lower lip. "Suck Lip," we'd called out to her, and she'd run after us, until her mother—Auntie—intervened raucously on her behalf.

I kept thinking how glad Goldie must be now because she always wanted to have a son. She was cuddling him, sore as she was and almost faint from her ordeal. Maybe too she was waiting for Verne to enter the room: to see their newborn; and there'd be gladness in her eyes, and in his as well.

Verne got up, then sat down again. I wanted to urge him on, to hurry into the room to greet Goldie. *To see his son!* Grandmother's lips twisting, her impatience growing. Verne continued to have an odd power over us, all because of the travelling he'd done. At times when he boasted about the outside world, he seemed to overwhelm Grandmother also.

Mrs Davis pointed to Verne. "Go an' see her, Verne," she urged, her words quick, rushed.

"Eh?" asked Verne, a ridiculous look on his face.

I suddenly wanted to laugh.

Grandmother looked at me; she seemed confused, yet resolute. Then she blurted out: "Go and see she—go an' see your wife Goldie, man. Go an' see your son too, eh? What you waitin' for?"

Verne seemed oddly confused.

Right then I figured Verne wished he was in Cuba, Moscow, or in some other faraway country. Yet, he also wanted to be here: close to Goldie and his child . . . his son.

He started getting up again, but his legs seemed weak. All the women, men, watched him; and really frail he looked, far unlike the one who wanted to transform the world by forming a powerful union of workers everywhere!

He went forward. "Is she . . . well?" he asked, looking at the women—as if wanting them to spare him further torture.

One fired back, "Yes, she okay. Is woman lot to go through wha' she just been through because of man's action!"

"Eh?" Verne asked. This immediately caused laughter. I also started laughing.

Maybe Goldie also heard the laughter, and was holding up her baby, muttering to it, because the infant no longer bawled. She was no doubt saying to her son, "See, they're all so happy, including your father."

The oil lamp sputtered, indicating a low wick. Grandmother drew closer to Verne. "Is a son you get; a really good child," she muttered.

"Go an' see how big he is, eh. Goldie done a good job. She been through a lot. You ask the women. Ask them all," and she looked at Mrs Davis as if wanting her compliance. The latter nodded. "Take good care o' she," Grandmother emphasized, like a pronouncement—a heavy weight from which Verne couldn't free himself, or else he'd be crushed by all the women.

I began to see Verne no longer travelling, but remaining at home with Goldie and his son . . . fussing over them to the amusement of everyone. And I heard Verne silently saying: "I want my son to grow up in a good country, where he can hold up his head high. An' be free of ignorance an' superstition, and . . . " But again Grandmother was looking sternly at him.

Strangely, I saw Goldie coming out of the side room in a whitish gown, assisted by one of the women; almost unnatural as this was: to be at Verne's side maybe. And the child?

Verne added haltingly, "You t'ink this country will remain this way forever? Things're going to change; we will truly govern ourselves, be masters of our own destiny. We will . . . " His voice petered out into a drawl.

Grandmother started laughing; and she was saying that Verne's travelling hadn't made him wiser; indeed, no one should ever leave his wife and child and mind other people's affairs, party politics or not. I imagined Grandmother and all the other women continuing to press down on Verne, heavily.

Finally Verne found the full range of his voice: "My son will have the best. He will. I will take good care of him!"

Again he looked at me, wanting my confirmation, approval, odd as this was. Next he looked at each of the men, and expected the same from them.

Then Verne declared he wouldn't travel again—all because of his son being born. Was I hearing correctly? I cringed, for I started seeing a new Verne, someone I didn't approve of: who stayed home only and wouldn't tell us about what was going on on the outside. Yes, Verne was giving in to Grandmother, and I didn't want this to happen.

I blurted out, "You must travel, Verne. You must!"

"Eh?" he replied, looking at me, then at Grandmother.

"If you don't, I will. I want to see the world in action," I cried.

Verne had a vague smile on his face, as if all the things he said in the past somehow weren't true. And what was the point of *transformation?* he was asking.

Goldie's eyes grew abnormally wide; and Verne was getting up and hurrying towards her, with everyone looking. Goldie, taking his hand, sighing, really exhausted as she was, yet her cheeks were flushed, and she'd indeed been through a real ordeal. Slowly, but deliberately, Verne was being led into the side room.

I waited to see Verne return with his son in his arms. Breathing hard I was, anxious. The midwife looked at me, then she laughed. "Ah, your time will come," she murmured, admonishing me, "Always remember you were a child once. Maybe you and this newborn goin' to be good friends. You too got fo' take care o' he."

"No," I let out. A new sensation stirring in me, with a whirl of thoughts. Grandmother grimaced.

"No?" asked Mrs Davis, humouring me now, smiling.

I pouted, petulant.

Verne reappeared, face almost white, as if he was afraid—the world-traveller and hardened socialist as he was. The baby was in his arms, he was cooing to it. No one laughed now.

Slowly, in a clear voice, Verne said: "You know what's the first thing Goldie asked me? You know what?"

We waited.

"She asked me when next I'll start travelling again. Ha, she asked me that!" He grinned. "Maybe she didn't want me near my own son." Again he cooed to the child. "Ah, so wonderful he looks, eh?"

Then Verne turned to Grandmother, adding: "Yes—Goldie asked me that." And just then Verne started crying, disappointing me no end; maybe disappointing all the men as well.

He added, "But I will stay right here! I will, believe me."

I figured Verne would keep his promise, as he added, "Yes, I will stay right here to be with my son." He was telling each of the women this; and one or two laughed, because Verne was beginning to look strange, even ridiculous.

Mrs Davis again went to the window to see more light coming in; and

I wasn't sure if it was really the sun or the moon she was looking at. And Grandmother was bidding the midwife goodbye, thanking her for her help. The other women were also at the door, the men close behind, all saying goodbye.

When Verne and I were alone in the living room, I said to him in a half-whisper, "You mean what you said 'bout not travelling again?"

He nodded.

"Tell me the truth, Verne." I demanded, looking closely at him.

He nodded once more.

"Well, maybe to the smaller islands round here. Trade union work, you see."

"But you're not a trade unionist, Verne. You're a politician," I argued.

He shrugged.

I looked out of the window, at the villagers going home; and maybe they'd be out in the fields in the blazing sun before long, because it was indeed a new day; these men and women perspiring heavily in their toil; and there was no way out really for them. The baby started crying again, almost with a deafening peal. But Verne was already hugging him tightly, and cooing louder.

Grandmother rejoined us, and she saw what Verne was doing and giggled like a young girl.

"That Verne, maybe he change fo' good," she said in a low voice.

"No," I said, suddenly defiant.

She wagged a finger at me. "You be careful. That Verne, he go mek you come out jus' like he. Wait until you start fo get pickney—you go see the difference!" Then you too won't want to become a prime minister."

I kept looking at her, while Verne's voice came loud and clear to me as he tried soothing the crying baby; and he was talking to Goldie as well, letting her know how he really felt.

Grandmother added, "Yes, you' time go come, eh."

Right then I knew what she meant, and I hurried back to the window. Looking out—far out—I began imagining myself a world traveller also . . . for I wanted to see everywhere else, all other countries. And strangely Verne's son was with me, the two of us going everywhere. And wherever we went, we were telling people of the workers' toil: telling them in no uncertain manner, including those in Europe, America, Canada.

Verne was standing next to me now and laughing—as if he didn't really believe it was a new day . . . his son's piercing cry still in his ears, confusing him maybe. And Grandmother was attending to Goldie and telling her about her own mother, then of a time when she'd first been a mother . . . which she cherished . . . but that was long gone now. Just then I saw Goldie's lower lip curl in, slowly—same as I always remembered—and burst out laughing.

The Pugilist

Slowly balling his fists, he would walk up to you, then *bam!* a fist jutted out to your face. Like a regular pugilist he was, and he'd knock you down flat. Laughter followed, and everyone figured they knew Mansingh's ways, mad as they thought he was or on the verge of becoming so. Sampat said, "Mansingh, clear yuh arse away," even as he looked at the fist close to his nose, eyeballing it; smelling it. But Mansingh's face was tight, lips set hard, fixed in his pugilist's stance like a newly erected monument, some said. Then slowly he relaxed his position, like a flower unfolding.

Mansingh went to the next fella: *bam!* And once more you could smell the knuckles; smell it even though you might be miles away. "Mansingh, is mad yuh playin' mad?" cried others, one sneering, then laughing. They watched the hold slowly relaxing; and Mansingh began walking away—as if he was the most harmless person in the world. It was all Mansingh's "madness," they said, and again they laughed harder.

It didn't take long for some people to start saying Mansingh was simply putting on an act; he was creating amusement in his odd way, though he never laughed himself, which in itself was strange. And they humoured him even more, stubbornly believing he was really harmless. But others started thinking Mansingh's supposed "madness" was the result of his being robbed by his brothers of his late father's estate: these brothers who were bigshots in the capital city, one a doctor, and another a lawyer as some East Indian sons ended up becoming—muttered an African . . . still laughing; and from time to time the villagers looked at Mansingh with a strange awe, marvelling that he indeed came from such an educated family.

When Mansingh took up his pugilist's stance once more, compulsive as he seemed, the awe seemed suddenly to disappear.

29

Another asked, "Is where he get that habit from, thinking he's a boxer?" A quick reply, "Worry over money does mek people turn out like dat."

"Strange, eh?"

Thoughts whirring in a general dissatisfaction, ennui, then sudden hilarity. "It like a calf born wid two heads, man," said Sampat laughing crazily.

"Maybe so," said another.

"People is people though, not cows," argued someone else.

"What difference it does make?" countered Sampat.

This would be repeated by the roadside, at culverts where people *limed* around, at the cakeshop, corner store, wakes and weddings. Everywhere else. Then, "It goin' to make a diff'rence when Mansingh hurt someone. You see how close he came to hitting Sampat on the nose," muttered another villager, genuinely alarmed.

"He gave Sampat the scare, man," cried another.

"Mansingh scare you boy! Heh-heh-heh. Dat man, skinny as an eel," chaffed someone else, pointing at Sampat with his mouth wide open. And Sampat suddenly looked embarrassed, eyes narrowing, upper teeth jutting out like short, sharp staves. Then: "Mansingh's really harmless," Sampat slowly said, as if he'd reached this conclusion a long time ago.

It began to be rumoured that Mansingh really imagined himself to be some sort of world-class boxer each time he stood before a fella with his fists folded. He kept playacting, being this famous boxer; at one time he was Sugar Ray Robinson, Archie Moore, then Cassius Clay. They overheard Mansingh muttering he was at Madison Square Garden in New York itself. "Oh God, man, he really goin' crazy!" cried someone else.

Maybe Mansingh was frustrated in his dream of becoming a champion. Now he was taking everyone in the village for ... a fool! But someone countered that Mansingh was really sad; he'd actually seen him crying when he was alone. No doubt Mansingh was thinking of his brothers robbing him of his share of the family's wealth; his pugilist's stance was really a kind of delayed reflex action—all that he intended doing to his brothers, though he couldn't even harm a fly.

Mansingh continued being a mystery as he walked down First Avenue,

Second, then Third, always appearing preoccupied, the fists slowly balling again.

Then someone said Mansingh would one day appear in a tailored, double-breasted suit, hot as the tropics were, and he'd be handing out American hundred-dollar bills like manna from heaven. Yes, wait and see. *Eh?* The bigshot he'd become, as if he'd just returned from America.

Another loudly hollered, "Ah tell you, Mansingh could become a bigshot wheeler-and-dealer. He wouldn't be the pugilist anymore!" This caused more crazed laughter to follow.

Mansingh started walking down Second Avenue, muttering to himself. A couple of pariah dogs followed, sniffing at his legs as the heat from the sun beat down relentlessly, making the dogs temperamental. And no one knew what Mansingh was thinking or saying to himself; maybe he was simply swearing at his brothers, or being just like regular mad people. Fellas tried recalling the names of other "mad" people in the district: Sulay, Jagabandoo. They jeered. Mansingh, they figured, was indeed mad. They laughed again and wanted to pelt stones at him as they taunted: "Mansingh, why yuh not go an' fight yuh brothers in Georgetown, eh?"

"Is money does mek East Indians talk to themselves like dat?" another hollered, East Indian as he himself was. Only vaguely the thought of East Indians brought here from the subcontinent a century ago to this part of South America flitted through their minds. Maybe East Indians were just like every one else: like the Arawaks, Caribs, Chinese, Africans, Syrians, and even Portuguese who'd originally come from Madeira, all appearing as one race, one people. In the Canje district, thoughts grew haywire. No one race seemed to prevail.

Mansingh, rigid as a pole, eyed the next one coming down the street. Immediately he started balling his fists.

"Don't play de fool wid me, Mansingh," snapped a fella called Snakie. He walked up boldly to Mansingh, taking up a pugilist's stance with a pretence of bravado.

Everyone laughed as they watched the two men square off.

Snakie's eyes hardened, determined, as he suddenly planned an attack; though in Mansingh's eyes, it didn't seem that way: everything was still unreal. Some also knew Snakie to be bad tempered, though now he was smiling, humouring Mansingh: a different Snakie altogether.

A small crowd gathered: boys, women wearing garish Madrasi headkerchief, men. Snakie snickered, then came more laughter.

Mansingh remained grim, lips tightly set, fists balled like wax in the fierce sun.

Snakie lightly cuffed Mansingh on the shoulder, as if he was a child as he said, "Man, Mansingh, I could knock you down in a second."

Mansingh looked like a mannequin in a department store, as he kept up his aggressive stance.

More kids gathered, laughing; they liked nothing better than to watch Mansingh in action, waiting to see when he'd let go that blow. Mansingh turned and faced them, fists tightening, still being the boxer. The kids laughed louder. Mansingh didn't laugh.

The crowd whirred like strange bees. The kids remained where they were, some also balling their fists and pretending to be Mansingh in mock attacks against one another. More laughter followed.

Mansingh wasn't seen around again for a while. Life in the village continued as usual: humdrum, predictable, nothing exciting happening. People arguing, quarrelling, the heat making them crotchety. The cane-cutting season started again, people becoming busier than usual. A bitch giving birth to seven pups which no one wanted. Then someone remembered Mansingh, asked about him, where was he now?

"You t'ink he dead?" asked another.

"Na. Mansingh go live up to a hundred!"

"Mad as he is an' all?"

"Yeah."

"Impossible!"

"Mad people does have no problems, nothin' to worry their mind."

"Someone go knock he down someday," growled another ominously. "They go t'ink he's for real."

"Heh-heh-heh, no one go ever tek he for real!"

They swatted flies away, and laughed again. One cuffed at a mosquito on his nose. "That Mansingh, he could be a first-rate boxer if he set his mind to it."

"You see his perfect stance. It just like a professional."

"Ha," came a reply.

"You see how he hold up his hands. And look at his legs, his fancy footwork."

"He fierce-lookin' too," came agreement. "If only he wasn't like he is, he could become a real professional." They were alluding to his mental illness.

More serious argument followed about how limited opportunities there were for people in the district: this like a new realization, one said; and how indeed someone like Mansingh, *talented* as he was, if he was born in America he'd be boxing champion of the world! Laughter again inevitably followed: this being too much for them to take seriously.

Mansingh reappeared, out of the blue almost; and fellas came around him at once, appraising him as never before . . . really imagining him a top-class boxer. One imagined him on the cover of *Time* magazine. No, it was too much to believe. Not the same Mansingh before them now; this could never happen, and they laughed harder.

Mansingh remained dour, seeming almost afraid. Slight tremor rose at the corners of his mouth. Then, as was to be expected, the youngsters started running behind him along the main street. Mansingh turned around a few times, glaring, squaring off at them. The kids jeered louder and squared off back at him, though safely, from some yards away. The adults, watching, also laughed, mindlessly.

"Mansingh, you go take on one o' them, eh?" hollered Sampat from an open window.

And still more laughter.

Mansingh slowly walked down Second Street. Women would now see him from a distance and quickly cross to the opposite side, anxious not to get close to him. Funny with women though: they also laughed the loudest.

But some were indeed starting to take Mansingh seriously, not taking any chances with him from the expressions on their faces. Maybe Mansingh walking along and balling his fists didn't discriminate between the sexes. To him everyone was a formidable foe.

Mansingh really put himself to the test one day upon seeing one of these very women with a baby in her arms coming down the opposite side of the street. It was Snakie's wife, Snakie's baby. The street was virtually empty, and the sun grew hotter. Mansingh walked up to her, with fists balled ... hard as iron, taking up his pugilist's stance. The odd thing was that Snakie's wife hadn't seen Mansingh come up to her. Then suddenly she saw him before her, and was scared speechless! And as if the five-month-old infant sensed the fear, he immediately cried out in a deafening bawl.

Mansingh, agitated by the bawling, suddenly hit the child with a fist right on the forehead.

Bop!

Snakie's wife screamed, as if a murder had just been committed. People rushed out from everywhere, from every house, every street: men, women, children.

Snakie's wife screamed louder, though the baby had stopped—he almost giggled at the excitement.

Everyone surrounded Mansingh, as if he was the biggest criminal they ever set eyes on. Mansingh looked dazed, keeping up his pugilist's stance.

"Mansingh—he hit the child!" bawled Snakie's wife. "Oh Gawd!"

"Where's Snakie? He mus' come quick!" someone else hollered. It was a nervous Sampat.

Every man, woman, and child appeared frantically to start looking around for Snakie.

Mansingh kept his fists balled, lips tight, even though if one looked closely he'd see abject puzzlement or fear in his eyes.

"Snakie—come quick!" yelled Sampat into another crowd surging.

"Mansingh murder yuh child!" cried another as Snakie shuffled closer, coming a few yards down the street.

Then Snakie charged in like a wild bull in action. Skinny like Mansingh, but muscular in the shoulder, and wiry, Snakie confronted Mansingh with a scowling glare. A few people at once smelt rum on Snakie's breath. He looked at his child's face, and he became even more agitated.

Then Snakie looked at Mansingh, whose fists were still balled ... and he knew at once what had happened.

Bop!

Bop!

BOP!

Mansingh, still in his pugilist's stance, felt his head snap backwards—like a heavy wind slapping it back.

The quickness of Snakie's reactions really surprised the people.

Though not Snakie's wife. "Oh Gawd, don't kill he now!" she cried.

"Don't hit he anymore, man!" someone else shouted.

Others at once joined in the general plea, to save Mansingh from sure death (as they said afterwards). But a few of the youngsters, who liked nothing better, let out:

"Mansingh, defend you'self! Let's see what kinda a boxer you really are!"

But another encouraged, "Hit him again, Snakie! One more time, hit him until he fall down! Rememba, he want fo kill you' child!"

This went on for another ten minutes.

All the while Mansingh said not a word. He merely remained rigid as a pole, the heavy wind slapping his head back.

The crowd slowly began to disperse, the fun being over. Snakie, half-drunk as he was, ushered his wife and infant home, a *hero*. It was noticed that this was the first time he had carried his infant in his arms. From time to time, almost tenderly, he patted the baby's head, his breath still reeking of rum.

One week . . . two weeks . . . almost a month later. There was no sign of Mansingh, and everyone figured he'd gone to Georgetown, the capital: he really belonged there, to live with his brothers who no doubt had taken sympathy on him. Maybe they'd eventually give him his rightful share of the family property (though none really believed this would ever happen). As before loud laughter came, everyone becoming relaxed. The women again laughed hard.

Snakie's wife, not long after the incident, saw a bump on the baby's forehead. She yelled out for Snakie, "Come, see, quick-quick—man!"

Together they examined the swelling on the infant's forehead: it was like an imprint, the result of Mansingh's blow, they concluded. They looked at each other and grimaced. The wind began blowing hard. The child giggled!

Los Toros

Headlights blaring in front of us, as we unzipped our flies and unabashedly pointed in the direction of the oncoming cars. One car stopped, and an attractive girl—as far as I could see—hair flying in the wind, gleamed with a smile. She waved, and instantly I waved back. The others, including Kaiso, Boyo, Chen—on their Raleigh bicycles—burst out laughing. *At me?* The car instantly sped off.

Los Toros we called ourselves, dressed in black slacks and red shirt—a bull embossed on the left pocket—and scented Brylcream styling our Elvis Presley hair; and in our zestful play we thought we looked perfect. Of course, other youths also formed gangs: like the *Argonauts;* but these were made up mostly of older boys, some grown men among them, all pretending to be ancient Greeks like Hercules and Achilles. And maybe we were expecting something ominous to happen soon, and were preparing for it, in our country, a new place. As we rode along the winding public road, that girl was still on my mind, long hair streaming in the wind, white teeth glistening. *Who was she?*

Now we felt we were no longer part of the British Empire, but were perhaps Hispanic, because we lived in a genuine Latin world. And we imagined ourselves talking in strange new accents, as we inhaled the tropical air and rode along, always with playful abandonment, pedalling harder and daring the world to tell us otherwise. Brazilians, Venezuelans, all others as we claimed to be, wilfully determining our destiny. Shouts, cries, with energy bursting out, our feelings stronger as we imitated an array of animals; the ocelot, jaguar, jaguarondi. Hinterland cats growled next, bloodcurdling; our baying at the moon. Next ancestral spirits echoed a past with Dutch and French sugar plantation owners . . . slaves buried with their white masters, going to the otherworld—and the slaves screaming out, not wanting to go under. Aaaaggggh!

Quickly I rode ahead of the others, pumping at the pedals, *Los Toros* as we were, always with a surge of youthful pride. Kaiso suddenly close to me: he'd caught up with me, breathing hard, his voice a rasp.

"What's the matter, Kaiso?" I asked, as we moved closer to the Anglican church, its spire rising high, with a wide cemetery adjacent—headstones sticking out like permanent sentinels. A saaman tree in the middle of the grounds, branches silhouetted in the moon's sombre light. Shadows, shapes, dancing eerily amidst thick brush. Zinnia mixed with rotten sugar cane and molasses smells filling the air, as we kept on going. A hundred yards away the giant cane factory hummed, throbbed, sometimes stupefying. Palatial-looking houses with well-manicured lawns owned by the sugar estate managers rose. Immediately we started another round of yells, stranger cries.

Kaiso, still close to me; and again I asked, "What's the matter?" Now he seemed in a world of his own, unlike a *toro*; and maybe our playacting was getting to him; he, now with a strange twist of his mouth, as the others kept up a din and yet talked about travelling far away from the coast: now from South America, the Caribbean.

Then Kaiso quickly rode past me. I decided to keep up with him. *Something was the matter.* The cries, sounds in the night air; something else riding past us too. That girl, somewhere, maybe still gleaming with a smile.

Another night: and we continued imitating animals, birds: tropical and temperate alike, screeching out what our imagination compelled us to shape; then, sounds of a running brook or a winding creek everywhere across the district leading to the vast ocean. Somewhere. All the while the factory hummed, in our sleep also; molasses smells heavy in the air. The large saaman tree still awesome-looking, as it stood by the cemetery close to the familiar-unfamiliar church.

Kaiso muttering again: about independence for our country. Ah, we were just fifteen-, sixteen-, and seventeen-year-olds—untested youths. But Kaiso seemed more determined, mouth twisting, nostrils flared, talking as if with a new rage.

"What independence?" I asked. We were yet Hispanic, genuine *Los Toros*, having fun, with our continuing zest.

"See them," cried the village women, pointing at us during the day, Madrasi headkerchiefs covering wide foreheads, against brown and black skin.

"Crazy, they are," others hooted.

"All crazy!" still others claimed, waving us off.

We stuck out our tongues, hissing: *"Los Toros! Los Toros!"* Then children, like cheerleaders, applauding.

A demure girl, African by her looks, turned to wave from a slope of ground near to the village well . . . not the same long-haired attractive one I'd seen before? Boyo, the tallest among us—the most handsome maybe—touched the embossed bull on his shirt, reassuring himself in readiness for small talk, applying his charm. The girl's quiet smile gave way to easy laughter. Boyo imitating James Dean, Elvis Presley, Paul Newman all in one; ah, promises to keep, in a rendezvous or tryst. The rest of us smiled widely, then really laughed.

Kaiso, still next to me, quoted an obscure statistic about the state of our country. Where he got his information from, I didn't know. Maybe I'd heard him say this before, and he wanted my full attention. Then he talked about war: the cold war. Next about a revolution brewing, somewhere. *Oh?*

"We mustn't be decadent," he rasped again. Did he mean about the girl and Boyo's love antics?

Kaiso's face narrower, as he sucked in air—looking at me. Then he berated us for pretending only; his hands shaking, determination in his eyes.

When I pedalled on further, he deliberately kept up with me. "We should be interested in real politics only," he grated. Kaiso was already a fanatic of sorts, I figured: all that he believed in, his face, serious manner, so uncompromising. Maybe he wasn't part of our gang anymore.

Next he said we should form a study group, because he wanted change. His lips throbbing. And again we were riding by the sugar estate compound: here where the *foreigners* lived.

I turned, looking back at the others, hearing Boyo cry out: "Girls are fun," then guffawing loudly into the night air.

"They're not," hissed Kaiso, to me. "We can get all the girls we want later."

Los Toros

"Later?" others reacted sceptically: they'd overheard him.

"Can we?" pressed Chen, also laughing—he the only Chinese among us, ready to explore all other possibilities.

Kaiso's features, lips a distinct tremor; and we stopped pedalling and stood before the giant sugar cane factory, enthralled. "This country's ours," Kaiso next muttered under his breath; as if there was any doubt about it. But the way he said it now, it seemed that the country never had been ours.

"The people here, they work for nothing." His eyes hardened with grit, malevolence.

"It will change," I said.

"When?" he shot back.

We looked at one another. I quickly shrugged.

Kaiso's mouth twitching, as he repeated: "You're all decadent! The whole gang o' you!" The look on his face tightening, and he didn't seem like the Kaiso I knew all along: close as we were, like brothers. "I'll leave *Los Toros* soon," he added, still tense.

I figured he meant it now. Yet I said, "You won't, Kaiso." Being in the gang was like belonging to a blood brotherhood: this thought filling my mind, as I contemplated our youthful determination, still feeling special because of the energy all around.

"I will leave," Kaiso hurled back.

Our *Los Toros:* Kaiso was threatening to break it up. Something, too, about strange news, the rumours, echoes: a civil war imminent because of the racial riots we kept hearing about. Did this have to do with our country recently obtaining independence? Again I looked at Kaiso—with a different imaginative pulse and frenzy; a different guise even.

Boyo, with his James Dean looks, kept on talking, boasting that he would one day date American move stars in Hollywood.

"Not French ones, like Brigit Bardot?" someone quipped.

Chen too boasting, saying he'd play tennis at Wimbledon before long: he, the tennis zealot among us. And we all wanted to go there to Wimbledon, to cheer him on.

"Could I join you there too?" asked Chris, the curly-headed one among us.

39

Chen laughed, in his face. "Wha' you want to go to England for? Is only for white people, not Africans." He affected a sneer.

"But you're not white?" retorted Chris. "You're Chinese."

"Chinese close to white people. see. Besides, I am a professional. And England's for professionals only, like me," Chen hooted.

"Ha!" mocked Chris, advancing in jest.

"I'll be the greatest tennis player, you'll see," Chen boasted.

"Not like Arthur Ashe?" drilled Chris, having the last laugh.

"Yeah, jus' like him," others chorused.

"You'd still get all the girls you want," said Boyo, red shirttail flying in the wind, the embossed bull like an insignia. He was preoccupied, fixated with girls.

Chen: "I'll travel to other countries, like Australia, New Zealand."

"Not Hong Kong?" asked Allim.

"To India as well?" pressed another.

Chen didn't answer, but I knew his thoughts were still on Wimbledon, always winning in his eyes. And maybe he now dismissed India and all other countries, as he laughed loudly.

Chris, not wanting to be left out of the boasting, said he'd be the best boxer—the best welterweight; even better than Sugar Ray Leonard. He'd box at Madison Square Garden in New York City, and he'd be on TV so that boxing fans all over the world could watch him—including fans in Mexico, Puerto Rico, Cuba. One day he'd be on the cover of *Sports Illustrated* itself!

"Like Cassius Clay?" I asked.

But another *toro* said that only cricketers were true sports heroes in our part of the world, among us. And those who played at Wimbledon were only the rich—they were never really heroes.

A new round of argument rose, and from time to time I turned to look at Kaiso, to see how he was taking it all, his face set firmly. Would he really leave us soon? I wanted him then to join in the friendly chaffing, the fun. But he muttered the word "Marxist": it was what he wanted to be. Was Karl Marx famous? I wanted to know, dwelling on this for a while.

"What about Lenin?" someone else whispered, as if privy to our thoughts.

A hushed silence all around.

"I will remain right here," Kaiso finally said; and the way he said this, he was still challenging me, us.

"You won't go to Cuba or Russia then?" asked Boyo, with a smirk.

Kaiso's eyes burned. "Wait and see. The time's coming; our country . . . " and he rode away again, pumping hard at the pedals; he wanted to be far away from us now. Was he still thinking of leaving us, *Los Toros*?

I rode hard to try to keep up with him. But it was no use; he seemed possessed of a demon speed. Behind us, following, the others continued laughing, Chen and Boyo loudest—regular *Los Toros:* thinking of other lands, other journeys, places afar. While I continued thinking about Kaiso; in a way I was getting worried about him. While the others kept on laughing, loud.

Kaiso headed for the Youth Centre housed in the People's Party building with its distinctly rickety stairs: a place sometimes smelling of dead insects, especially in the inside stairs leading to the second floor where the main hall was located. Here, from time to time, "important" speakers came, giving the place a sense of serious goings-on. Young politicians who wanted to change the world also came here.

"I'm not a member," I told Kaiso when I joined him there. "I shouldn't be here, you know."

He frowned. A new side to Kaiso now; and maybe he came here alone sometimes, didn't he? A finality in his voice, manner. At once I wished the others were with us. The hall empty, as Kaiso started moving the chairs around, a little nervously. Then he pulled one chair in front, alongside a narrow, oblong table. He intrigued me now. Next he sat down at this head table, and closing his eyes, he concentrated. Then he rose to speak before his imaginary audience.

"Ladies and gentlemen, comrades and friends," he began, "imperialism is the cause of our malaise." Hands chopping the air, his maiden speech begun, his expression rigid, dour, uncompromising as he was.

He talked on for the next twenty minutes, lips pursed, captivating his "audience" as he gesticulated, imagining more and more as the words literally rolled off his tongue. He continued to lambast imperialism, colonialism; and maybe all our woes would soon be over when he finished his "speech." Ah, his eyes rivetted to his imaginary audience, and names like Castro, Marti, Guevara followed. Other names, revolutionaries . . . his hands still chopping the air. Was he still a *toro?*

Kaiso sighed, and stopped speaking. Then he asked: "How was I?"

"Not bad."

He pulled up his collar so he might look older, suave. "You think I could make our country independent?"

"We're already independent."

"The expatriates still own everyt'ing."

I was frightened by his tone, as deadly serious as he looked.

I nodded, to please him. I didn't want him to leave our gang. The others' jeers in my ears, Boyo's especially.

Kaiso grinned. "I mean it, you know. We're living in a time of turbulence."

"What?"

A perplexed look on his face, hinting at the riots in our country, and further political dissension yet to come. And foreigners taking over again—meaning the British and Americans.

He repeated, "I mean it. I will drop out of the gang."

"What for?"

"I don't want to pretend any longer."

"We're not pretendin'."

His face tightened, mouth narrow. He moved closer to me, and rasped: "This country will remain like this for a long time."

"What d'you mean, Kaiso?"

He started repeating some of the things he said earlier in his speech, about imperialism, capitalism. Then: "You should learn more about politics. It's the only way. Don't be decadent."

"The only way?"

I waited. He didn't bother to explain further.

I too started practising making speeches; my hands chopping the air in front of the mirror at home. Then I began laughing, saying, "See, I don't believe all you say, Kaiso. I don't."

When we rode out again, I listened to the others, critically, for the first time: it was Kaiso's impact on me, his speech.

Chen still thinking about Wimbledon, imagining a crowd applauding him, he said. Boyo's black hair neatly combed back, the irrepressible James Dean that he was, muttering: "That Kaiso, he thinks about politics night an' day. He's not having any fun. Maybe he's not like us any more."

"We should have a purpose in life," I crowed.

"Like Kaiso?" Boyo baited, looking grim.

"We have to save our country."

The others laughed.

Chris added, "Boxing is all," then rode off, letting out a loud whoop, a yell, all in the cane-scented air. Now, where were Brazil, Venezuela— all the other Latin places? I kept thinking about turmoil in those countries, also; and maybe they had youths like us too. This thought compelling, with the politics; and I figured I had to find Kaiso. At once. An urgency, desire for change—something new whirring in me; all because of my listening to Kaiso speak to his imaginary audience at the Party building.

Kaiso, where was he? He wasn't around now. He didn't come with us the following night, and the night after. Strangely, I started thinking of our people as never before: the villagers around us, who hailed us often; the other gangs, also. My silent rumination, determination: it was as simple as black and white; and why were the others in our gang not seeing it so clearly? My hands again chopping the air, with images of the workers' gnarled appearances, rough skins. Kaiso still talking, making another "speech": and I was still at the Party Building, listening to him. After he asked: "How was I?"

I began laughing: laughing at myself.

Then I decided to join a study group, one that Kaiso had mentioned before. A few heavy volumes: all that Kaiso carried with him under his arms, which he displayed on the head table; and where he got the books from, I didn't know. One volume had a picture of Marx on the cover. Another seemed to be about strategy and tactics, written by Lenin himself—I thought: nothing would go wrong under him! Kaiso smiled. "Socialism, scientific socialism, is the answer."

Then I didn't want Boyo, Chen, Chris, Allim, the others to listen to him, or else they'd laugh and spoil the mood. Loyalty kept me to Kaiso:

we were *Los Toros.*

Kaiso started reading whole passages from one volume, repeating Marx's name, then Lenin's, his eyes gleaming. Next he commented on each passage, asking those present—three others—to interpret for him what he read, and to doubt Marx or Lenin if we dared! I knew then that when we rode out as a gang, it would never be the same again.

After, Kaiso muttered, "I know what you're thinking."

"What?" I said.

He flipped through the pages of one special volume, then looked at me, and maybe he was disappointed in me.

I didn't want him to feel this way; I still wanted us to be friends, because we were *Los Toros.* I also wanted to believe all that he said about political change; but maybe I was taking a long time to come around to his way of thinking, his ideas.

He grimaced.

The next day there were five new faces at the Party building, all who'd joined our study group. Kaiso said he'd been expecting them. Once more he set about reading select passages, here and there: Kaiso imitating Marx or Lenin, perhaps, by the way he read, his voice rising; though at times he seemed confused and fumbled his words.

I tried to force a deeper interest in politics, revolution.

Someone asked, "Is Marxism a dogma?"

"No," Kaiso shot back. "Just a—"

"A what?" quickly demanded another.

"Guide to action."

Kaiso had a ready answer for everything, as he looked at me and smiled. Suddenly I wanted the other members of our gang to be here: to hear him read and explain things. To hear him *expound*; and immediately I wanted to laugh. Then I figured that by our being here, the two of us—with these *others*—we were betraying *Los Toros.*

Someone entered—someone new—an older man: grave-looking. Kaiso said he was the teacher. A deferential air filled the hall, and Kaiso had been expecting him all along, hadn't he? This "teacher" was supposed to have travelled: had been to Moscow and to other Eastern Bloc countries. He'd been to Cuba as well. Eyebrows raised, as we looked at him, at his smooth complexion, calm, confident manner.

When the "teacher" began speaking, his words seemed effortless, so articulate he was as he talked about capitalism dying in America. No thought of Ronald Reagan yet to come . . . no hint of Gorbachev. Yes, the balance of forces in the world was changing, didn't we know? The collapse of the Soviet Union was far from his mind, unthinkable. Dialectical materialism seemed all: this analysis, logic, absolute. Look at Africa, Latin America . . . the teacher declaimed with rhetorical flourish, yet solemn. "Look at Angola, Nicaragua, *comrades!*" Eyes darting, as he spoke; then he became calm, looking at each one of us, penetratingly, as if he expected us to go out and change the world right away.

Why just then I didn't like him, I didn't know, yet I kept my eyes rivetted to him, then to the heavy volumes.

Indeed Marx had predicted it would happen this way, he added, soundly rooted in socialist theory as he was, and as he wanted us to be.

Kaiso came to me in a corner and muttered, "What's it now?"

"Nothing." I was tightlipped.

"We're still a colony, you know." He sensed my growing scepticism. "What difference it make?"

He ignored this.

That evening we continued our double life being *Los Toros,* going around for the usual ride (we who had secretly been attending Party lectures). Kaiso now staying farther back, or sometimes quickly riding ahead, so unpredictable he was. The others didn't ask anything about him now; and I became disappointed.

Then I figured Kaiso would much rather be at home reading his large volumes, always managing the heavy-sounding phrases with a dictionary close by. Indeed, politics was his life. Yet, I wanted Boyo—he more than anyone else—to talk to Kaiso, decadent as Boyo was; maybe we all were. Boyo would perhaps make Kaiso have some fun—as much as he was having.

Chen, too, always outgoing as he was: I wanted him to talk to Kaiso. Mohan and Ramesh also, laughing, teasing. But they all seemed to want to leave Kaiso to himself. Chris pursed his lips . . . maybe he was still thinking of entering the ring in Madison Square Garden in New York.

Once more we started making sounds, echoing hinterland voices, crying out, or baying at the distant moon. And we were jungle cats: the jaguar, jaguarondi, ocelot, once more, until we became exhausted.

For a while I forgot about Kaiso. Then I sensed his handle bar almost touching mine, as he asked, "Can you hear them coming?"

"Who's coming?"

A nervous fear in him, and maybe the others at the Party building, the "teacher" especially, were now making him afraid.

"The animals . . . they're here," he said.

I stiffened.

Closer to the sugarcane factory, the throbbing, grinding sound reaching a crescendo; and I rode closer to Kaiso. Suddenly he seemed ready with his best raucous notes . . . as we neared the expatriates' quarters. Then absolute silence . . . a strange prescience in the air.

All eyes were now on Kaiso, as I inhaled the smell of rotten cane mixed with mollusc, crab, shrimp; the stench of manure, composts of dead leaves; bootleg rum rampant amidst an ancient, lingering smell of desiccated insects, reptiles. And trade wind wafting, with the iodine of the close-by sea. Night's darkness lengthening, the clouds forming like large bolts of cloth, rolling and unrolling as we rode on.

Rain started falling, thick drops coming down, then thrashing sounds: the ground leaping up as the drops pelted, kicked up veritable clods of earth.

In the darkness, we quickly rode for cover, as thunder rolled. All other sounds, smells, diminished, disappearing. The sky's blackness gashed by the white face of lightning. Where was Kaiso? He'd become separated from us during the storm . . . and now I wanted to find him.

I decided to go straight to the Party Building: something troubling my spirit, my instinct, goading me.

As I expected, Kaiso was there. Alone he was, practising another speech. The rain was kicking up the earth, rivulets, the streets being overrun. Kaiso's eyes burned as he talked, staring at me. And again I started thinking about *Los Toros*: all our hopes with Chen in Wimbledon; Chris, Mohan: with their individual dreams, aspirations in foreign places. And now no one wanted to work in the sugar plantation, or to go to neighbouring Latin America. The raindrops' *plop-plop-plop*, like tennis balls hitting against the boards. Were they all listening?

My turn to practise a speech. I pulled the collar close to my neck, as Kaiso had done, imagining myself a maverick, a debutante.

I expected Kaiso to start laughing.

He didn't.

"How do I look?" I pressed, my vain gesture akin to parody. He grimaced. I pulled the collar higher, closer. All of a sudden Kaiso laughed.

I also laughed.

His turn to pull up his collar, and he asked, "How do I look now?" Kaiso was his old self again.

"Like a gangster," I mocked.

He laughed. "Not like Humphrey Bogart?"

"Maybe like a prime minister," I replied.

He seemed pleased, as he pursed his lips, face crimsoning: such an odd expression; and all I was able to mutter to him was: "You wastin' your time, Kaiso. See, you're not the same anymore—not like a *toro*!"

His lips merely tightened: that was all.

The newspapers blared it out: we'd been expecting it, an invasion; as if coming right after the heavy downpour of rain. A dark pulse of voices, whispers, people huddling before their radios—the few that existed—listening to the news in fear. And protests seemed to be talked about everywhere, though everyone was cowed. And it was as if political turmoil and racial violence were overtaking the country: all one inexplicable knot of twisted feelings, marred politics. Ah, we were trapped by a particular destiny; bizarre too it seemed, and it couldn't be real. Maybe Communism was everywhere now, it was also rumoured. Kaiso, I thought: Was he safe? Why wasn't he coming to see me? Soldiers from England, the Coldstream Guards—the same who guarded the Queen in Buckingham Palace—they were here! Then another rumour: these soldiers were really US marines, the Green Berets no less. More horrid looks on our faces; and we all were literally under seige! *Los Toros* would indeed be disbanded, disappear; we wouldn't ever be able to go out at night because of a curfew: we'd no longer give rein to our emotion with coastland and hinterland voices. And the whole of Guyana, the Caribbean, Central and South America . . . were under attack!

Kaiso, he suddenly took on a new importance the more I thought about it: he became busier than usual, I could tell, either planning or attending some meeting. All hush-hush. And why I began to feel left out now, just when I wanted to become more involved, I didn't know. Newspaper headlines, and the radio still blaring out the invasion . . . all because of this *thing* that was among us and which had to be stopped. *Communism!* The teacher's cool tone, he'd hinted at an invasion, hadn't he? Fear gripped me.

A knock on my door; our house shaking, the beams quivering in broad daylight.

Nervously I opened the door.

It was Kaiso. I was immediately glad to see him. He looked agitated, his expression florid. He came to invite me to a special meeting. He didn't look me in the eye.

Then he tapped me on the shoulder. Yes, I was also a freedom fighter, just when I didn't want to be one.

"You must come," Kaiso encouraged, almost brash. "We got no choice."

"But Kaiso . . . " I began.

He put a finger to his lips, indicating silence, secrecy. More would be said later, tonight, at the meeting. I thought of his last speech as "prime minister," collar pulled up, yet looking like Humphrey Bogart. I wanted to tell him about that now; but he was gone.

How I longed for our entire gang to be together: Boyo's laughter, care-free; Chen talking about Wimbledon and tennis balls cracking hard as he slapped the racket in passionate, intense play. Chris the pugilist still at it. The evening air, balmy; greetings from passersby because of the "fame" we'd cultivated; my contemplating the bull embossed on the pocket of my red shirt, its fresh significance, meaning. New sensations kept going through me, memories also, with the sense of belonging, my growing up—and always places we wanted to go to, I wanted to go to.

I took my time to get to the Party Building, looking left and right all the way.

Climbing the stairs, slowly: Who else would be here now? No sound, no one else; not even a slight bustle. Then it dawned on me that maybe the entire gang would be here. Chen, Boyo, Chris, with fear in their eyes:

Kaiso had indeed gotten us all together, finally. And there were others too, many whom I hadn't seen before. The teacher with books on the front table, volumes with Lenin's face prominent.

Kaiso smiled, pleased to see me, amidst the books' overwhelming presence, all their own.

He got up and began speaking, gesticulating, a fiery pitch to his voice. Yes, imperialism was at work. Then odd his voice started sounding, his tone; he'd gotten it from a good source that we could still be free; we didn't have to remain here under the seige by the combined forces of Britain and America.

Oh?

He laughed nervously . . . unlike himself, his face a pantomime, lips curving in. Yes, some of us could also go deep into the hinterland and remain there for a while. To *plan a guerilla attack!*

I rubbed my eyes. The others fidgeting, Boyo more nervous than the others. Instinctively my hand moved to touch the bull on my shirt pocket, lightly tapping it.

Kaiso was also looking around. Something in the air. A collective tension growing, becoming palpable, ominous.

The door suddenly burst open. Soldiers—bayonets sticking out— rushed in, six or seven of them, though it seemed like a hundred. Each grim-faced . . . as if from another planet they were: this was the actual siege, invasion, wasn't it?

In the midst of our shock, I glanced at Kaiso, and maybe he seemed pleased, a wide smile on his mouth.

The soldiers looked at the heavy volumes on the table, and more than one seemed intrigued. My thoughts raced.

One really tanned-looking soldier close to me sighed, blonde hair bristling. And maybe he too was nervous, as he looked at us, at me. Another picked up the book with Lenin's face on the cover—and slowly turned the pages. Then he looked around, at me again. The red shirt I was wearing; no one else was wearing theirs. Red signified *revolution*, no?

Eyes again focused on the picture of Lenin. Now each soldier was looking at it, then turning to look at me: Who was I? Kaiso also looking at me, no longer smiling: and he now appeared unlike a *toro*. A strange taste entered my mouth. My shirt indeed, all the soldiers coming towards me—the revolutionary, terrorist, diehard communist!

Kaiso would save me perhaps. Silently, mutely, I called out his name.

But he was fading into the background; and the soldiers' eyes still bore holes into me, their bayonets piercing my flesh, the bull itself, gored. *Blood spilled!*

Laughter, loud, clear: everyone was indeed laughing, including Boyo and Chen. Were they laughing because of the expression on my face?

The soldiers' mouths widening, expanding like rubber it seemed. Boyo was laughing louder: still at me? And maybe they knew I wasn't a revolutionary, wasn't a communist.

Kaiso, he was the only one who wasn't laughing. His face crimsoning, only; then I saw him instinctively pull up his collar, and move towards the door, looking like Humphrey Bogart indeed!

Boyo and the others were suddenly pointing at him, and laughing harder.

Right then I knew it was the end of our gang, the end of *Los Toros*; the end too of our wanting to be a part of other places, regions, the continent. We'd eventually go our separate ways, travelling to England, America, Canada—only.

Kaiso, he being different, would no doubt go to Eastern Europe, or Cuba. Chen's eyes glinting, a tennis racket in his hand, oddly pleased because the soldiers he was looking at were from England, ha! Chris still at Madison Square Garden putting on his gloves and squaring off . . . against a former Green Beret?

One freckle-faced soldier picked up the Lenin volume, gripping it, muttering something to himself, and maybe still laughing.

Quietly I retreated into myself, thinking of the animals we often imitated, coastland and hinterland: all their sounds locked in my throat. Suddenly I wanted the animals to go after Kaiso . . . to stop him, prevent him from leaving! But Kaiso kept on going away, the collar pulled higher and covering the back of his head like a hood. I stood my ground, the laughter still coming from Boyo, Chen, Chris, the others. The freckle-faced soldier drew closer to me, and maybe he too could hear the sounds, the vicarious animals, the hinterland spirit. And who was I? He started smiling, maybe already asking.

But I was only thinking of Kaiso outside, where he was now; and the rain was again pelting down, resounding; as everyone else started going down the rickety stairs leading to the main door on the first floor to the outside: as if to a far country. The walls, streets, echoing. Headlights glaring, and that girl passing by, her hair streaming in the wind, pointing at me. *Or was it at Kaiso . . . by himself . . . alone?*

Delsa

"See, it's Delsa coming," one cried. "Delsa, you remember her?"

"Yes, that *one*!" came an answer, with a smirk—then immediate laughter. Peering through windows, jalousies, they were, everyone looking out for Delsa coming down the street. Delsa, sultry yet appearing brazen as she lifted her head, a strange expression in her eyes: and something about Delsa when you looked at her made you want to swallow hard. Thin, yet pretty with thick eyelashes and long jet-black but lustrous hair, all uniquely East Indian—Delsa now seemed *different*. She'd been living in the town, and to the village diehards, her name now sounded unlike an East Indian's: it was associated with loud music and close-up dancing. But other district girls from staunch Hindu and Muslim families were also rumoured to be heading for the town—all hush-hush—some younger than Delsa, who was in her twenties.

"Yes, look at her good—Delsa coming indeed!" said another, with a snicker, peering out further from the window.

Delsa, as they all knew, when the whim seized her, would return to the village hoping to "make good" with her parents, especially with her father Balgobin—if that were ever possible. Maybe she regretted having left the village to go in the town to live "that kind of life," almost three years ago. And some of the women watching Delsa felt superior, though they also reflected on the freedom she had away from strict family codes and village morals imposed by the diehards. Now, prettier than ever Delsa looked: with her lipstick and rouge, an assortment of face creams, exotic cologne; some watching her could inhale her fragrance. Delsa appeared to bring the village and the town closer.

They studied the knee-high cut of her dress, the low neck; and Delsa oddly now gave them a strange power over their men, as they giggled embarrassedly at this thought.

Balgobin, Delsa's father, then Sumintra, her mother, also noted Delsa coming down the street. "Why she disgrace we like dat," murmured Sumintra; she meant Delsa leaving home and living in the town. Balgobin sulked.

Delsa quietly but deliberately walked to the family home, pretending everything was normal. And girls—ten-, eleven-, and twelve-year-olds, some older—quickly came and surrounded her. Delsa fussed about them, smiling. And the parents immediately worried about Delsa putting thoughts into their heads, ideas about the town mainly.

Sumintra said to Delsa when they were alone, "Why you na want fo live like the rest of we?"

Delsa shook her head, as if to say: *What's the use? I'll never be accepted here again.*

Balgobin—a rancher, sometimes smelling of wet rope and maybe a whiff of cow manure—remained glum. Delsa forced a grin, looking away from her father. Balgobin growled to his wife, "Why she come?" His tone always scolding.

Sumintra moaned. "Ow man, she's we own child." Her voice one of sustained regret, always meant to please Balgobin.

Balgobin grunted.

The younger girls kept frolicking, really happy Delsa came home. "Maybe she won't come again," added Sumintra with impatience, out of Delsa's earshot. "She'll never get married too," Balgobin retorted, reflecting on who'd want to marry a prostitute and how Delsa was doomed to a life without a husband, without a family of her own.

Delsa's younger sister Rohini, hearing her father's insult, ran off to cry in a corner. Yes, Delsa was her "dear sister" who always brought her large quantities of hairpins, combs, brooches, laces, things one easily obtained in the town—with which Rohini would make small dresses with special frills decorating them all.

"Stop crying," scolded Balgobin.

"She go come again—you'll see," said Sumintra to Rohini, conciliatory, as if Delsa had taken off back to the town again.

"Eh?" snapped Balgobin, mouth hardening. Then he glanced at Rohini, for whom he had a soft spot. It was a pity Delsa turned out the way she did, though in a way he was resigned to her black sheep status.

Sumintra muttered, "Ow man, Rohini is she sister."

Delsa stayed around the house, chatting, smiling with a few of the neighbours, with her sister Rohini and other young girls; now and again she muttered a few laconic words to her mother; all the while Balgobin kept his distance. And for a while everyone seemed to forget about Delsa: they talked about the upcoming labour strike, the politicians and rigged elections, and always about people leaving the country, everyone hoping to come to Toronto or New York one day. Once in a while someone mentioned Russia or Cuba, which aroused laughter.

Another ventured, "We people can also go anywhere if we set we mind to it."

"Poor as we are here in this country?" asked a sceptic.

Another hurled, "Is not rich people only that can travel!"

A strong gust of wind blew, smelling of the cowshit that was sometimes used to daub the bottom-house where women gathered and sat on empty brown sugar and jute bags. A stronger wind wafted more agreeable smells of black sage, acacia, hibiscus, and zinnia. An array of flowers hung pendulant on the hedges around the village where hummingbirds, emerald-looking, dazzled in the bright sunshine. Insects, wasps darting, dodging; the dragonflies almost iridescent; as the women kept on gossiping, about Delsa once more. Rohini, like a skittish young horse, ran in and out of her parents' house.

Then word passed around that Delsa had come home this time to announce she was getting married. "To whom?" came the question, as it seemed impossible that Delsa would marry.

Rohini tittered, as Delsa continued smiling; and it was like a big secret Delsa had stored up in her, which she would now slowly divulge; ah, something she'd been savouring for the right moment. Again the women asked, incredulously: Who would marry her?

Balgobin to his wife Sumintra, reflected on this also. *Who indeed would want to marry Delsa?* "Ow, is we own child. We should be happy for her," countered a sympathetic Sumintra, careful not to annoy her husband.

Then Delsa took off again. The wind wafted stronger smells, with jasmine, lime, ochra, mango in the air. Rohini giggled endlessly, as she received the adulation of other young girls admiring the beautiful lace decorating her hair, cheeks. She even jeered, making a face—a really ugly face—and cried, "Delsa, Delsa!" and laughed happily.

Everyone kept an instinctive lookout for Delsa: when she'd come again, and who'd be with her. Rohini teased them, "I know who you lookin' for. Is DEL-SA!" she sang, lace dangling from her hair. "Or is someone else?" she laughed. Only twelve, Rohini seemed precocious, understanding of adults' ways, their many lies, and she laughed again.

"You want to see who she go marry!" Rohini clamoured next.

"Ow, Rohini, you playin' big-people," came a curt reply. Another chuckled, then chided, "Maybe is a slap you want, Rohini."

These harsh words sent Rohini running to her mother in tears. Sumintra—not one to let an insult go by, went arms akimbo to the neighbour, just as Rohini wanted. But Sumintra didn't advance further.

Rohini, still feeling the insult, decided to lock herself in her room and started crying—and imagined . . . Delsa coming home with a husband to confound them all! Yes, what would he be like? Someone weird-looking, or even a decrepit old man? She cuffed at her pillow, and said she hated everyone—all of them outside. Maybe she too would leave the village and go to the town as Delsa did! Sumintra gasped. And more tears rolled down Rohini's cheeks.

"Rohini, come out of that room now," cried a distraught Sumintra. "At once!"

Rohini thought next she'd one day go abroad—to be far, far away from everyone.

"Rohini, you hear me? Come out! Or else I will tell your Pa!" Sumintra knocked on the door.

"Go tell he. See what he can do!" Rohini fired back.

"Oh me God, Rohini—come out from there!" bawled Sumintra.

Rohini kept on thinking of one day going abroad—if only Delsa could help her.

"You will turn out just like Delsa—wicked," hissed Sumintra, unforgiving.

"Delsa na wicked," Rohini shot back at the keyhole.

"Wha' you say?" screeched Sumintra, unable to cope with the insolence. "You got hotmouth!"

"Delsa'll get married, you'll see—just like everybody else."

After a while the door slowly opened, Rohini coming out with her head bent, tears still coming down her cheeks . . . and then into her mother's waiting arms.

Sumintra said consolingly, "You differen', you na like Delsa."

Rohini sobbed, and leant closer to her mother. Then she lifted her head—as if she was now in command. And she started telling her mother how one day she'd travel, and maybe she'd make the family proud. "I will go to England or America and maybe become a doctor or lawyer, Ma."

"We na gat money, child," muttered Sumintra, smiling at this sudden ambition .

"Delsa go give me money."

"Eh?" Sumintra's jaw tightened.

"She rich!"

"How you know?" A heavy frown crossed Sumintra's angular face.

Rohini shrugged, and playfully muttered, "She go marry a rich man, a rich townman."

Sumintra raised her eyebrows, the innocence she thought she often saw in Rohini was no longer there, and it frightened her.

Rohini added, "Delsa done tell me. She will give me the money her townman-husband'll give her. Then Pa goin' to be really proud of me."

Sumintra wrung her hands, looking away, then turned to look at Rohini again. "You really want to go to England?"

Rohini brightened as she smiled. And so didSumintra, as she hadn't done in a long time because she never thought Rohini would have such thoughts. She added, "You really want to go to 'merica so your Pa'll be proud of you?"

"To Englan'. Yes, Delsa will give me the money, she and she townman," said a determined Rohini.

That night in their room Sumintra and Balgobin, awake, stared up at the ceiling. Then Balgobin growled, "You really think Delsa go marry someone?"

"Man, Delsa is your child. It's our fault she turn out like that," said Sumintra.

Balgobin turned on the other side of the bed.

Sumintra wanted to tell him about Rohini's ambitions, and how much Rohini admired her older sister. Instead, she listened to Balgobin's heavy breathing—like someone who'd become seriously ill.

Sumintra added, "Where you t'ink they'll live after they marry?"

"Who?" hissed Balgobin.

"Delsa and her husband—who else?"

"Not here!" snapped Balgobin, the thought worrying him.

"Where then?" moaned Sumintra, her thoughts on Rohini again.

"She belongs there, not wid us," Balgobin said, looking up at the ceiling in the semidarkness.

A lone firefly hummed, buzzed.

"Yes, she'll live in the town among those people she accustomed to—those who live like cat an' dog," added Balgobin, alluding to loose living among Africans, Portuguese, Chinese, Syrians, and other mixed races that Partied and danced all night with hifi music and spent lavishly on food and drink.

"We're no better," Sumintra said, surprising him.

Balgobin turned to face her—he thought she would explain herself.

Sumintra kept silent.

When Delsa came again, she indeed brought someone with her—as was to be expected. He was about her age, shy, handsome, definitely not dissolute-looking. Tony, Delsa called him and smiled, showing him off to the neighbours who crowded about him, some eager to talk: to see if, perhaps, he was somehow flaky for wanting to marry someone like Delsa. Then casually Delsa said that he was already her husband, which caused more amazement. Tony remained quiet, almost solemn. And more neighbours came to see Delsa's husband, some treating Delsa as if she were some sort of prodigal who'd suddenly made good.

Tony shook their hands and repeated "Thank you" to everyone.

"How was the wedding?" another asked.

Delsa grinned, very polite, as if taking a cue from her husband. marriage already had an effect on her, which was why she wasn't boastful or loud as they might have expected her to be with her "catch." Then Delsa said the wedding was something small: a few friends, a cake, expressions of happiness—a real Christian ceremony. *But Delsa was a Hindu, no?* Eyes turned to Balgobin, who dourly glanced at his son-in-law, but didn't look at Delsa, though he wasn't impolite. And maybe he was glad that Delsa was now married—at last she had *"cleared his name."*

Sumintra muttered to him, "Yes, man, now your daughter married, so don't feel ashamed anymore." Then she started fussing about Tony, like a dutiful mother-in-law. Balgobin looked from Delsa to Tony, then to Delsa again.

Sumintra primed Tony's plate with food, showing hospitality to such a "nice boy"; and casually she asked questions about his background, his family.

But Tony said little, as Rohini chirped about him, then about Delsa, talking nonstop. Delsa rather matter-of-factly muttered, "Tony and I will be goin'—"

"Going?" chorussed everyone, all ears.

Delsa smiled, looking around, taking her time. "Goin' to America," she said.

"To America?" came disbelief.

Rohini nearly jumped for joy.

All eyes appraised Delsa afresh: the same girl who'd grown up among them, who'd moved to the town to live an irregular life . . . would now be going to America, unless it was a joke.

Delsa assured them it wasn't. America was a place she'd always wanted to go to; and she looked at Tony who nodded and smiled. She added that America was the place of higher education, art museums, interesting people, where new and exciting things happened. She dumbfounded them with what she already knew about America: what she no doubt picked up from living in the town. And they looked critically at Tony, thinking it was his influence over her. Even Balgobin looked at him this way.

"Yes," beamed Delsa, "Tony an' I will really be goin' there."

They looked at Delsa's husband and blurted out: "Is it true?"

More than one were hoping he'd say no; that Delsa, well, she was only kidding.

Tony merely smiled, politely.

"America is so far away," another said, not sure how else to respond. Delsa continued beaming, like someone indeed having the last laugh. And Tony remained steadfastly quiet, as they reassessed him—thinking he was indeed handsome, intelligent. "It's my idea," Delsa added, reading their thoughts. "Tony doesn't want to go to America, but I convinced him we should." She laughed. Rohini laughed next to her, giddily slapping her shoulder.

Balgobin watched Delsa, not without grudging admiration—thinking of people who'd gone to America and Canada and after a while returned looking prosperous—so changed they were. He imagined the same happening to Delsa—his daughter—skinny, wasted almost as she'd seemed, though pretty. Maybe when Delsa returned she'd outdo them all for beauty.

Delsa looked at her father in turn, and beamed further. Rohini grinned from ear to ear. A neighbour plaintively murmured, "Is good you goin' to 'merica, eh. Things too bad now. Politics make things rotten here"—which sounded like a general lamentation.

Balgobin turned to his wife, who said she was pleased at how things were turning out. She added, "He's a really nice boy"; she was surprised when her husband nodded.

"They suit each other," she went on.

Balgobin didn't nod this time, though he was thinking how much he really loved Delsa as a child, the pride of his life: and how sad he became when she'd taken off to live in the town.

Rohini came and sat close to her father, as Balgobin started wondering if Hinduism was ever practised in America. He glanced at Tony talking with the younger girls: the latter suddenly seemed to have lost their village shyness. Now Balgobin wanted to go to him and shake his hand, awkward as this was. But he stood his ground.

"What you thinkin', man?" egged Sumintra.

Balgobin shook his head. "Nothing."

"You should be proud of your daughter."

They were both irascible; and Sumintra again turned and looked at Delsa, then at Tony, and muttered: "He not say much, eh. Maybe 'merica go change him. It like that I hear."

Balgobin threw a sceptical look at her. "What you really hear?"

"In 'merica everybody is talkative. An' they have loud music every-where too," Sumintra said with gusto.

"Jus' like in the town where Delsa been living all this time?" he ma-liciously reminded her, as if suddenly it was her fault Delsa had left home that first time. His thoughts were in a maelstrom as he added, "Yes, Delsa belong there; that's why she's taking him *there*!" He stam-mered, stumbling with his words.

Balgobin felt more confused, as Rohini still chirped around, again rushing from Delsa to Tony.

"How can you say that now?" scolded Sumintra. "She's your own daughter."

"You forget how Delsa disgraced us?"

"Ow, man—that's in the Past now," Sumintra almost pleaded, still fearing her husband's wrath.

Balgobin kept on simmering, looking at Delsa laughing with the neighbours: just as when she was a young girl.

"You gettin' old, man," Sumintra accused, then smiled ingratiatingly.

"Eh?" he barked.

"Delsa will now take away our shame."

He merely said, "Maybe is good she going to 'merica."

Sumintra wasn't sure what Balgobin was thinking. "Eh?" was all she said, as if in reflex action.

"So I won't see her again," he droned.

"Man—you crazy," she snapped. "You want to spoil Delsa's happi-ness. You should now be glad."

"'merica not mek me glad," he growled.

Tony drew close to him; and Balgobin with difficulty asked: "You t'ink dis 'merica is a good place fo' you?"

Tony glanced in the direction of the now-talkative Delsa. "She thinks so," he said, pointing.

"She think so?" Balgobin almost mocked. "Why d'you allow her to be in command?"

Tony added, "She's always been like that."

Balgobin stared at his son-in-law, and he kept dwelling on the word *always*, and again reflected on the Pain Delsa had caused him by leaving home—though so long ago. He looked at Tony, then at Delsa, who was still laughing; and he started imagining Delsa in a faraway place, in New York City amid neon lights, skyscrapers . . . a place with millions of people no doubt. The images, busyness, making him feel immediately insecure, a simple village man as he was.

He whirred, with Tony looking at him.

Delsa kept on laughing all the time.

Balgobin ground his teeth; as Tony quietly moved back to be close to his wife and to mutter something to her, then he too started laughing. Balgobin rubbed his eyes in amazement.

Sumintra said, "Look how they're happy together." She waited, then added: "You t'ink of something to give them." She was referring to custom, a dowry maybe—before their deParture.

Balgobin rasped, "I don't want her to go anymore!"

"Wha'?"

"She mustn' go!"

"You crazy, man."

"She belongs with us!" The intensity in his voice really surprised Sumintra.

"Man, you disown she a long time ago," Sumintra said, toying with him in a way.

"Never mind that," he snapped. She waited to hear him add, incredulously: "She's my . . . *daughta!*" The words forced out in a hoarse, dry tone, and he was also red in the face.

Sumintra politely looked away, muttering, "Yes, I love Delsa too, man. Just like I love Rohini." A tear glistened in her right eye.

Then they both looked at Tony, as if he was the mysterious one, not Delsa. And maybe they wanted some kind of concurrence from him— even as they heard Rohini's highpitched laughter again.

A sixth sense in Delsa, indicating to her the strange feelings in her Parents, as she muttered:

"Maybe you can come an' live with me and Tony in America. You'll see what it's really like there."

Balgobin and Sumintra looked at her a little stunned.

Delsa added, "You'll see something else, different politics, different people." She looked directly at her father, at how his eyes were crinkled and red.

Tony drew close by too, watching them.

Balgobin again started thinking about their Hindu traditions. And it seemed the world was changing too fast for him, as he blinked and let out an unconscious laugh. Sumintra tittered like a child. Rohini came now and held her father's hand, gripping it earnestly, saying, "You see, Pa, we must go. Then I'll study hard to become a doctor or lawyer. I really will!"

Balgobin looked at her in amazement, considering her audacity, precocity. An unaccustomed tightness had gripped Rohini's mouth, the veins on her neck were tense too. And was he expecting Rohini to start laughing?

Delsa smiled, and with Tony next to her she seemed full of a radiant beauty. Tony took her hand and began leading her away.

Balgobin looked at them, and quietly he began experiencing a strange freedom, something new in his spirit; and the past no longer gnawed at him: as it had done all these years. This new spirit floating up in him, he felt, as he looked at Rohini too . . . then again at Delsa and Tony walking away, *going to America*! And unconsciously he started reaching out to them, then imagining himself patting Delsa's face, head. Rohini instinctively moving next to her mother and leaning against her breast, he noticed, as both women kept smiling, all the while.

The Outsider

B-52 bombers were raging over North Vietnam, all of Southeast Asia; but here, in the woods of Northern Ontario, an insistent *rat-tatting* seemed all. The woodpecker's bill kept hitting hard against beech bark, as I lifted the tree-planting shovel across my shoulder, vicariously aiming at the unseen enemy—and fired! Exhilarated I felt, breathing in the fresh air amidst spruce and jackpine. A new day, new season, and, now I was glad to be here, though I didn't look forward to the weeks of back-breaking work of planting trees ahead: ploughing through muskeg and thick brush, and fending off blackflies fat as fists and mosquitoes long as fingers. Trapper Lake, not far from the giant Lake Superior, also felt like the centre of the world: my being here with an odd group of Aboriginals, winos, foreign students, American draft-dodgers—the latter sometimes a noisy, raucous bunch: Mickey, Steve, and Duke who was distinctly bearded—who swore heavily and sometimes laughed louder than the rest. These sounds echoing in the forest; and, again, r*at-tat-tat!*

Once more I lifted my shovel, aiming at the unseen enemy, firing. Someone watching me, and slowly I turned around.

A tallish, stringy youth, pale-looking—resembling an acolyte who'd just stepped down from the altar—was staring at me. He sensed my playacting, the shovel in my hand. He wasn't like the other Americans, I figured.

We shook hands, and after Harry surveyed the burnt-out area around, though he also looked up at the woodpecker as it kept up its constant rat-tat, bits of white birch bark falling or flying about. He smiled, and muttered something about having come from Washington, DC, and his father was a major in the army. "Bastard," he let out under his breath, gritting his teeth. Clearly Harry was against war, the Vietnam War: his father's involvement in it perhaps. Harry, I figured, would be planting next to me, amidst the others' guffaws: Mickey, Rick, Duke still at it, boisterous as ever.

Harry quickly scuffed the topsoil, and bent down to plant the jackpine seedling in his hand into the ground. Then he tugged the young tree to make sure no roots stuck out and, satisfied, he looked at me and smiled. In June weather, the heat began to slowly rise, and it'd become humid after a while. Harry gulped in air and wiped perspiration from his face, neck. Mosquitoes, blackflies swirled, and I handed him the fly repellent, the thick grease I rubbed on my arms, neck, face and other exposed parts of my body. We talked from time to time as we worked, now some distance from the other crew members; and he said he'd changed his last name: he no longer wanted to be called Anderson . . . but *Singh*.

"Singh?" I echoed, the East Indian or Sikh name on my lips, which I knew meant "lion". A thought of my ancestry, distances. I looked at him, waiting for him to say more.

Harry mumbled something about being a member of a commune or sect living in the outskirts of Thunder Bay, not more than sixty miles away. Other Americans were living in communes in the area, I'd heard. Mickey, Steve, Rick, Duke also? Maybe they were all against the Vietnam War; and riots, protests, across America. In Chicago. And in Canada too. Elsewhere?

Almost disdainful Harry looked, wiping sweat off his face, muttering something or the other; he said that in the commune they made candles, which they sold for a living. Watching me to see how I was taking him, he added that the *Mother* at the commune was a strong leader, deeply religious: she instilled the virtue of hard work, and now she wanted them to try other ways of bringing in money. I imagined someone with long, jet-black hair, cascades of it, reaching down to her hefty breasts—a woman who was distinctly matronly. Yes, she now wanted them to plant trees, and Harry, still an initiate perhaps, had agreed.

"Ever planted trees before?" I asked. He was breathing hard, his hands thin, his fingers like tendrils, gentle.

"Nope," he said.

I whipped out the next seedling from the bag on my shoulder carrying almost three hundred spruce and jackpine. The Ontario Government was making sure the region wouldn't become deforested after the heavy logging by giant paper companies. Harry sneered at that; and, after a while, he seemed preoccupied. An Ojibwa planter laughed not far from us; another let out a wild whoop; something defiant in the air; in Harry too no doubt. Something lingering. The other Americans laughing again, I heard, and it felt as if we were all now in no-man's-land here so far from Washington DC, New York, California . . . Vietnam! Harry made a face, and continued talking about the Mother: he wanted me to know everything about her, now insistent. "You may think I am a fanatic of sorts," he murmured. "Maybe I am," and then smiled. He'd heard the talk going around about a Hare Krishna sect, and it didn't bother him. *Was he one?* Then he muttered about the war in Vietnam, and he seemed suddenly enraged, his mouth twisting, ugly.

I nodded, again considering distances; then, the woodpecker's sounds once more; and, in the mood I was in, I was still firing at it. Then, stepping over heavy moss, twisted, gnarled branches, logs, lichen crawling on slabs of stone in this hilly area, we literally clambered up, and down again to plant the trees among burnt-out areas, charcoal edges.

Harry said he was tired, and so was I. Oddly, the thought crossed my mind again that Harry wasn't really suited for tree-planting (maybe I wasn't either); and was it because he was now talking about transcendental experience: his eyes closed, as he sat cross-legged on crusted greyish stone, muttering a mantra? He intrigued me, the American that he was; and maybe he was curious about me too.

My own background: my parents' religious beliefs—he wanted to know about—and my features, skin colour. He asked about India, as if I had come from there; and I muttered something about South America, and an indentured past. He looked more curiously at me, from time to time, and, maybe he smiled. Recollecting my mother's pujas, I was . . . and the jhandi ceremony performed, far away: my childhood, my growing up. Incense in the air, ghee burning, as I crinkled my nostrils. My mother's eyes closed, deep in concentration, piety: all her religious manner, belief. A symbolic red flag strung on top of a tall bamboo and placed in front of our house in faraway Guyana: as part of the ceremony. Money, gifts for Krishna kept in a tightly knotted kerchief— the red flag really— fluttering for weeks through rain or shine. Clouds piling up overhead, all the tropics' own. *And did the red colour of the flag really signify heaven?*

Harry muttered that they were all vegetarians at the commune, the Mother insisting on it: such was the discipline, creed. Ah, this time of the late sixties turning to nineteen-seventy, with more social ferment. Anarchy. And I was here, not removed from it, being far from home.

Harry continued on about discipline, karma, a life of devotion; and not all the Americans at the camp lived in communes, he said. Not all were draft dodgers. The others' louder cries coming to us above the cedar trees, and the hard work here in the forest yet to be done: the crew bosses insisting on it, determined.

Harry slapped mosquitoes away from his arms, neck, with a marked irritation. Then he was eager to tell me more, about the Mother offering them the genuine spiritual path. Was she from somewhere in Asia? He was against all forms of violence, a genuine peacenik he was, and he smiled: with an aura of blissful ease and innocence amidst the flies, other insects thickly hovering.

Again on a slab of stone he sat, his legs folded under, the taller trees untouched by the fire wavering, fronds fluttering across the scarred terrain, landscape. Harry kept muttering: another mantra or prayer . . . invocation to an ancient god perhaps, one which I felt removed from, yet suddenly close to. Harry smiled, being the acolyte all over again: this image, this beginning perhaps.

That night huddled in small groups by the campsite, we were; a radio blaring out the news of bombing in Southeast Asia. President Lyndon Johnson, the Berrigan Brothers, Jane Fonda; and it seemed as if all time had suddenly collapsed . . . all events were one across a far distance. A heated argument quickly rose, part of the general anachronism. Harry and I listened in frenzy, flux. The Americans had no right being in Southeast Asia. Duke, berating, pulling at his beard like limp wires. Another becoming agitated: it all began to feel like an illusion.

Curses, groans. A loud, uninhibited fart. Someone flaunting a hundred different patches on his jeans—psychedelic he called it—a real hippie still, as he talked obsessively about setting up rabbit farms all over the Third World. Rabbits multiplying quickly in his head, in every village, town, in Asia: it'd solve the problem of hunger and starvation in the Third World!

"That's bullshit, man," cried Duke. Another fart, lugubrious. A Chinese foreign student grimaced next to me.

A Cree named Redbird sniggered. Harry closed his eyes, as if he was back in the commune, close to the Mother. *Rat-tat-tat,* guns firing. Once more I was aiming at the unseen enemy. Birch bark flying everywhere.

When we planted again, I told Harry I was trying to work my way through school. He grimaced. He was planting a few yards ahead of me now.

My shovel raised, playacting, as I yearned for relief from the drudgery of planting trees; the sun burning my skin, yet resplendent it was against the leaves, tree trunks: the surrounding pine and spruce. Harry—he wanted to rest again; the flies were bothering him. Then, suddenly, he started taking larger steps, still planting. I noticed other planters behind a cluster of taller trees near a burnt-out spot about thirty yards away. Then I looked at the remaining trees in my bag, counting what was left to plant in this really back-breaking work. But I needed the money, the work had to be done. More blackflies and mosquitoes swirled about me, and I cursed. Instinctively I began drawing closer to Harry.

"It's good meeting you," he said, a ringlet of the sun's rays haloing his face, his cheeks dappled, pale-looking as he really was, so white.

"Me too," I said, acknowledging his friendship.

"Purifying the soul is what I want," he hummed. A mammoth hush, the forest's overwhelming silence all around. We wouldn't plant much more for the rest of the day, I figured. Yet Harry continued on, moving slowly ahead, and with each tree he took painstaking care, as I yet tried to keep close to him. I made sure no roots stuck out of my own effort, each seedling firm in the ground; I tested each with a slight tug, and no strong wind would blow these away. I imagined the smile of satisfaction on the crew boss's face.

From time to time I looked across at Harry. His bag was still almost full. The blackflies and mosquitoes were disappearing, yet I rubbed more grease, fly repellent, around my neck, ears. And it felt hotter than usual, but the heat didn't deter the planters. Now everyone would try to finish their trees before; and sometimes the Natives finished planting first, then the Americans: Duke, Rick, Mickey; everyone knew the latter *stashed* trees, burying a whole bundle of twenty-five at a time. Their laughter again rang out. Another woodpecker, somewhere, *rat-tat-tat*. I raised the shovel to my shoulder, perspiration sticking to my neck, almost burning. *Firing*.

Harry, maybe the heat was getting to him now.

When I handed him the fly repellent, he refused, muttering something about strength, perseverance. The Mother? Far away, South America in my mind, the red flag fluttering on the bamboo pole . . . *heaven*.

Harry still drifting apart: as I reflected on all he'd said about belief. I started assessing my own attitude to the spiritual life; and my mother's instinct and sense of faith, with little impact on me.

Closer to Harry I moved, though he didn't see me because of brush separating us. I noticed that most of the trees in his bag were gone. I decided to look more closely.

Then I saw him put a whole bundle of trees—all twenty-five—into the ground in one swift, smooth movement; so adept he was at it. Then he planted a solid tree on top of the buried bundle, tugging it, deliberately testing it to make sure the tree was well-planted. Harry was indeed *stashing* trees!

Smiling to himself, he moved away from the "spot," as I kept watching him. Into the open, in a clearing, Harry let out, "Phew," and breathed in in a falsely laboured way. "Hard work this," he said, looking into my bag which was still half full. He made a sick face. "Here, let me help you."

"No, Harry," I was still thinking of the trees he just buried.

"Let's take a break."

"Not now, Harry."

"You sure you don't want me to help you?" He looked into my bag and moaned. Then he walked away, maybe to start meditating again on the spiritual path.

A little later I heard a crack, someone nearby, the footsteps coming closer. It wasn't the other planters, I knew; they were some distance from us. The sound louder, and I became more curious. Harry? What was he up to?

Then I saw one of the crew bosses coming towards me. "Where are the others?" asked Bob. "Why aren't they planting the fucking trees?"

"They're finished planting, I guess," I said.

He looked around at the trees planted, then started scuffing the topsoil, so determined he looked. "That's strange," he muttered.

"What's strange?"

"That Jesus-freak, Harry—he finished too?"

I shrugged.

Bob looked surprised, an odd grin gashing his face. He glanced at my bag, reckoning there were more than a hundred trees left to be planted. Then he surveyed more of the ground where Harry had planted. Quickly he started pulling up dirt with his bare hands; he was looking for buried trees. He raised his head, mouth twisting, looking at me.

"It's no use, Bob," I tried.

Then he pulled out a bundle of trees from under a freshly planted spruce. He couldn't be fooled. He smiled: as if to say, *I told you so.*

The other planters kept up their loud laughing, being cheerful, somewhere in the background. Bob didn't bother about them now; only that bundle in his hand, as he looked around with a determined glare and still surveyed the ground, thinking no doubt that scores of trees were buried everywhere ... all Harry's? I figured he was now out to get Harry.

Bob pulled out another bundle of buried trees. "I'd seen him before," he said, solemn. "Been watching him, you see. The Jesus-freak."

"Jesus-freak?"

"Yeah, Harry."

"Are you going to fire him?

"Shit, yes."

Really heavy tramping sounds we heard, the ground being pounded. Bob looked at me, and we gingerly moved close to a thick clump of rhubarb where the sound was coming from.

We saw Harry there, moving about in a semi-circle, a million black-flies, mosquitoes around him, his face a blotched, black mass, and he was writhing. Where did all the insects suddenly come from? Then Harry started running around in a full circle, as more insects came at him. Vaguely I thought of a rainforest, the tropical coastland I'd left behind. But that seemed illusory now, it was the past. An immediacy, urgency was all this instant.

"Let's help him, Bob," I cried.

Bob grinned, fingers tightening round the last bundle of trees he'd dug up.

"Come on," I yelled, moving closer to Harry whose reddish-white face was really a mass of blackflies. Only the whiteness of his teeth shone.

Harry started hollering, so much in pain he was. I ran closer, and tried reaching out to him, despite the thick knot of insects flying around. I dodged a dozen, moving sideways. But Harry waved me off.

"Leave me alone," he cried, as if he'd gone berserk. It seemed he deliberately wanted to get eaten alive by the insects. Oddly, his words about self-discipline, karma—all came back to me in a flash.

Other planters quickly drew near, including the Americans. Duke made a sick bearded face. "He's really a freak, man," he cried.

"This guy's fighting flies like they're his enemies," cried another.

I looked at one American carrying a "grenade," which was ready to go off in his hands—he said—the bundle of trees tightening at his wrist.

I focused on fat welts appearing on Harry's face, arms and neck. The crew bosses were supposed to take care of the planters—it was government regulation. Now this was a real emergency, as Harry fell to the ground, still writhing, rolling around and calling out, "Mother! Mother!" Next he was uttering curses—a long list of them. Someone laughed—it was Mickey.

"Oh God, help him someone!" Bob cried, frightened by what was going on.

"Mother, Mother," mumbled Harry, rolling on leaves, grass, burnt-out logs.

Other planters ran helter-skelter, one to get the first-aid kit. Maybe they'd ask the bus driver to rush him to a hospital, which was almost fifty miles away. *Incredible!* Bob continued to look terrified.

Harry suddenly turned and looked at me, and a determined expression filled his face; then, he seemed as if he was smiling. But he was in pain: he couldn't fool me.

"We must get help," Bob repeated, looking around in dismay.

"He needs an ambulance," someone else hissed.

"A what?" snarled Steve, another American, unsympathetic.

"He's in great pain," I said. "Just look at him." I turned to Bob, who appeared even more confused. "Goddam, let's do something before it's too late!" Then Bob dropped the bundle of trees he had in his hand, and ran for help.

Harry's face started changing its shape—it seemed—and more and more he looked unlike himself. He kept on writhing, moaning. "Hey, man, this is far out," cried Duke. "He's one of us—an American."

Three or four others started lifting Harry, and I assisted. But Harry kept moaning loudly, resisting us, eyes opening, closing in quick succession.

I wondered how long it would take for an ambulance to get into the forest; and how long it'd actually take to get Harry to the nearest hospital. Then Harry opened his eyes again, and he remained still. Deathly still.

Oddly I still recalled his religious talk, his serene life at the commune, the Mother preaching to them: about faith, belief only.

Then nothing else seemed real, here among the trees, with only a shrill rustle from time to time: the wind coming through the forest. A woodpecker's *rat-tat-tat*—somewhere, louder; maybe not far away.

I leaned close to Harry. "Hey, it's me—your partner," I said. "Can you hear me?'

Harry's lips pulsed, mouth opening a little. I figured he was in terrible pain. "Can you hear me, Harry?" I asked.

His lips moved slightly. He muttered, "Mother . . . Mother."

Duke, Steve, and the others frowned.

"Mother, Mother," Harry muttered again. The others looked around askance.

Bob returned with a first-aid kit, two other crew bosses with him. "How's he doing?" Bob asked.

"Shit," another crew boss let out upon seeing Harry's blotched face. "It's that bad, eh."

We successfully lifted Harry onto a makeshift stretcher and carried him to the bus about fifty yards away. And I kept hoping he would open his eyes again. Bob, in the meanwhile, regained his poise, his aplomb. He was in command once more. Harry would be taken to a hospital right away, he said.

I'd like to go with Harry, I said .

"What for?" Bob barked.

The trees have to be planted, he added, as he looked around at the other planters—the Americans, with suspicion in his eyes.

Duke rubbed his thick beard in disgust. I figured Bob was thinking of the many trees *he* too had buried; then he looked at Harry again with an expressionless hate. Harry, suddenly, opened his eyes.

We watched him in the bus, and I tried to get a good look at him through the window. The bus started taking off.

Now I figured Harry wouldn't be returning to plant trees again. Maybe he'd return to Washington D.C. to be close to his father, army major and all; and the Mother maybe would continue chanting, somewhere in a Northern Ontario commune, the Hare Krishna sect perhaps as it was, but being against the Vietnam War nevertheless . . . blackflies and mosquitoes still humming and resounding in the forest, with a strange echo.

Rat-tat-tat. The war raging on. More American bombing: in Cambodia next; or maybe in all of Southeast Asia.

Louder cries of protests across America. Riots. Burning. Looting. Jane Fonda in rhapsody, clamouring on campus at Kent State University. Elsewhere. And coming to Canada to speak. I recalled, listening to her with a strange rapture my own not so long ago.

A forest fire again, charcoal residues becoming topsoil.

Rain that night at camp at Trapper Lake. And imagining that before long a new tree would soon be forming roots, turning up the underground soil. My shovel in place, lips throbbing; the woodpecker once more I saw, as I kept listening for it, always.

Duke tugging at a new tree he planted, then scratching his beard and muttering close to me, "It's incredible he pulled it off like that."

I looked at him. He meant Harry, of course.

Higher I lifted the shovel, aiming because of the woodpecker's noise coming closer, but seeming everywhere in the surrounding forest. I also heard the bus trundling along, with Harry in it—and he was looking back at me; and I wouldn't see him ever again, I thought.

Rat-tat-tat.
I fired.
Duke laughing loudly, across the entire forest.
FLIES!

All for Love

Marco was at it again, talking loudly, his voice coming clearly to my room at one-thirty in the morning. Infuriating, maddening: and I couldn't sleep. How could anyone? Marco's face, like a cherub's, lips oddly puckering and making everyone downstairs laugh; he was really likeable, if only he didn't talk so loudly at night. Sometimes I'd go down to the kitchen and remind him there were others in the rooming house who wanted to sleep. Didn't they? Even tell him that Canada wasn't like Brazil—all that I imagined Brazil to be: a sustained carnival, revelry, all night long.

Guyana, I knew, wasn't far from Brazil: it was noisy there also where I'd been born, but I'd been living in Canada a long time now, I'd become *Canadianized*; and Marco had laughed when I told him this. "You're just like the English, *amigo*," he hissed.

This night, the noise continuing: Marco's seeming agitation, fuss. Getting out of bed, I walked down the stairs, as the voices floated up to me: more animated, ejaculatory. I was starting to get angry.

Seeing me, Marco rushed forward, eyes shining, his shortish figure appearing much shorter in the 90-watt kitchen light.

"What's de matter, *amigo*. You no sleep?" Apologetic, smiling: he knew he'd somehow awakened me. He plied his charm, then pretence of naivete. A sustained grin on his face; ah, I was one like *them*, still an immigrant, no? Remembering I spoke some Spanish, he asked, *"Tienes dormir?"*

"No, Marco." I was determined not to let him get away with it. "You're making too much noise; this is Canada."

"Canada?" and he laughed, mouth opening wide like the gills of a large fish. Then he winced, shaking his head, becoming almost doleful. Maybe something was genuinely wrong the way I said "this is *Canada.*"

74

He kept looking at me, head a little lowered.

But I was still nursing my anger; I wanted to sleep.

Marco kept me glued to him, his smallish head moving left and right, face in a slight tremor. "You know," he added, still agitated-looking, "police came . . . not too long ago."

"What for?"

I knew that from time to time police came to the house here not far from the the Voyageur Colonial Bus Terminal; it had this reputation, but it was the first place I took upon arriving in Ottawa, figuring the capital city would be my home, my destiny sort of. Not Toronto, Montreal, Vancouver; here where I figured I'd be close to real Canadians, the politicians, top level bureaucrats (called mandarins, as if I were in pre-revolutionary China): people with power, who ran everyone's lives across the country.

"Benedito, *amigo*," Marco held me, dramatic. "He's gone; they've taken him away!" Marco and Benedito had shared the same large room downstairs for the past three months; I'd often see them together, the best of pals. They lived in the same village in Brazil too, no doubt, outside San Paolo not far from a crime-ridden *favela* he'd told me, oddly with a strange gleam in his eyes.

Benedito seemed the taciturn, shy type: he hardly ever said much. A few hand gestures, that was all; maybe he didn't speak a word of English (or Portuguese for that matter). Yes, I knew they'd talked about living in Canada for the rest of their lives: their gesticulations and all, so excited they were by the prospects. And I figured I too had come to Canada for the same reason, like thousands of others from around the world who kept on coming. And now Ottawa, a once staid place, was beginning to change with West Indians, Italians, Lebanese, Portuguese, Vietnamese, Chinese, all here among the French, the British. But who was prepared for the likes of Marco?

"Why did they take Benedito away?" I asked dully, vaguely thinking about the police.

"Immigration . . . he's been working illegally. See, they found out," Marco's eyes lit up, upper teeth protruding, spittle forming at the sides of his mouth. He seemed disgusted as he added, "I know what you're thinking, Why not me too, eh? I too work *illegally*. Like Benedito, I also clean rugs."

I waited, light flickering from somewhere. Where were the others in the house?

"Yes," Marco kept on at it, "we work very hard, from morning to night."

Then he let out a mocking laugh, as if all he was saying was now somehow unreal. "I wasn't at home, *amigo*," Marco still muttered. "Only Benedito—he came home early. Ya, the *policia*, maybe they followed him here." Eyes widening, as he looked around, a little furtive.

"Benedito's my *bess* frien'. He *iss* going back to Brazil, eh?" Marco added. I urged him to say more, my anger about not sleeping slowly disappearing.

"He make enough money in three months, more than he makes three years in Brazil," went on Marco. He scratched his upper lip, the tip of his nose, and when he smiled again, his teeth shone as in an advertisement.

"You know," he murmured, looking around, "I've been in court once. They ask me, 'You work illegally?' Me? I no understand English. *Much*o confusing. I shake my head, I tell them no. But I say I come to Canada to start a new life. Maybe I not come just to make money like Benedito!"

It was then that I noticed the tallish, heavyset man standing in a corner, leaning against the door, watching Marco as he talked.

Marco added, "My wife, well, she jus' nineteen when she died . . . in *childbirth*. That's how you say it? You speak English well, yet you from South America too? Ya, maybe you speak English too fast for me. Maybe you do well in Canada, no?" He looked doleful again.

The other merely listened, like a strange shadow. Who was he?

"I learn English in Brazil, some of it," Marco continued. "I try to speak it more now in Canada, that's why I came here." He wanted my approval. The other suddenly rasped a laugh.

I looked from Marco to the heavyset man.

"Hey," said Marco, realizing he hadn't introduced me, "meet Albert, he too *iss* Brazilian. He's citizen of Canada, ya, jus' like you. Albert's been living here a long time. Good, huh?" Marco seemed nervous now, yet still ingratiating.

Albert leant against the door, largish head dominant, unsmiling. He could easily pass for a bouncer in a downtown bar, his expression surly, his face one that intimidated easily.

I yawned, pretending not to be intrigued. Now it was getting to almost two o'clock in the morning.

"You like Brazilians?" Albert hissed.

I felt compelled to say yes.

"You like Pele too? Great soccer player," Marco chirped. "He play soccer in America too. He's black, but they treat blacks like . . . " He couldn't find the word, his face tightening. "Like *SHEET*," he spat.

Albert grunted.

"But Pele does well, doesn't he?" I asked.

Albert muttered dryly as he looked sideways at Marco, "You keep liking Pele. He's Brazilian—never American, see. Never forget that!" It sounded like a threat.

I was in no mood to complain. I forced a yawn.

Marco ignored my annoyance at having been disturbed by his and Albert's loud talking, their lamenting Benedito's fate maybe and expressing their own nostalgia for Brazil. The door of Marco's room ajar, and my eyes strayed to a battered-looking photograph conspicuously placed at an angle: a picture of a girl.

Marco caught my eyes' focus , and he ran into the room to fetch the photograph, quickly handing it to me and declaring: "This *iss mi esposa, amigo*—my wife! She died, I tol' you!"

I studied the forlorn face of a thin-looking girl, maybe eighteen or nineteen; I vaguely recalled a niece who'd also been married young, long ago, who'd wanted to come to Canada but couldn't afford the plane ticket. I muttered, "You didn't tell me this before, Marco."

He handed the picture to Albert—maybe the latter hadn't seen it before. My thoughts going back to South America, the village weddings in Guyana, other parts of the Caribbean; the festivity, sometimes unrestrained joy.

Albert handed the picture back to Marco, impassive, and he again grunted. Then he was ready to leave, and moved towards the door. But Marco rushed after him, jabbering at him in rapid-fire Portuguese; then his voice became a shriek in English: "I want to remain in Canada, ya!

I must, I don't want to go back there! I love dis country, nowhere else. But it's not a crime to work illegally! Maybe they'll send me back too, like they send back Benedito!" It was as if Marco was shouting the words to all of Ottawa: especially to those on Parliament Hill only three or four kilometres away from where we were. And he indeed wanted all of Canada to hear what he was saying, imploring.

Albert walked on.

"Benedito's a soldier back in Brazil," cried Marco. "Maybe he will go back to become a *soldado*, no? Remember, we're jus' like brothers, he an' I. Maybe he come back as a landed immigrant too!"

After a while Marco started laughing, like a strange madness about him.

I rubbed my eyes, again feeling somewhat sleepy. A bus now leaving the terminal across the street, another coming in from somewhere else at this late hour. The door closed behind Albert, and Marco, in a lower voice, said to me:

"Albert *iss* my bess friend too, you know. He comes from the same *ciudad*, Rio, as me. He *iss* good man, like all Brazilians, ya!"

My mind vaguely set on rain forests, all the talk of the environment, Amazonia, on TV, radio, and saving the planet because of the greenhosue effect. Was it only the responsibility of Brazilians to save the planet? Yes, Benedito, Marco and Albert—all asking, What about others? I allowed a slight grimace to form on my face.

Marco looked at me and laughed again.

"Maybe I believe Albert, eh? He says he'll never become a Canadian," Marco added. "He works same place as me, as a supervisor. *Iss* hard to tell sometimes wid Albert though." Doleful again he was, the photograph in his hand, as he looked at it: that girl, his wife, dying while giving birth to their first child—he said slowly. A lingering memory, sadness. Closing his eyes, Marco was also getting tired.

He yawned, and I did the same.

Somehow I continued thinking about Albert, his dour, even gritty, appearance. I thought about Benedito also. All because of Marco's presence with me. I met Marco in the kitchen two days later. He seemed hearty, eyes twinkling." Guess what?" he said, close-up, leaving no personal space between us: my *Canadianized* way, no?

"What?"

"I'll get married again." Grinning from ear to ear he was.

I quickly looked into his room for that picture of his *esposa*, vaguely recalling the beautiful slim-waisted girl, their wedding picture; a crowd of well-wishers, confetti thrown in the air; a car revving up, hurrying away, bride and groom together: Marco with his wife going off on a blissful honeymoon far, far from a favella, eager to start a new life. Cheeping sounds of the rainforest, an echo, remembrance.

"I will get married to Albert's sister," Marco said, "He will be good brother-in-law, and maybe after I stay in Canada forever. I too will become Canadian citizen, ya. Not like Benedito?" He laughed disdainfully.

I tried recalling Albert's face, demeanour; broad-shouldered and heavyset as he was; his grave, unsmiling manner.

"Yes," Marco added, then appeared distressed as he drew closer to me—watching me, wanting my approval maybe.

I nodded.

"Say, what's de matter wid you? You no like me to marry again? It's three months since I been wid a woman. Ya, I will be a Canadian citizen too, one day." The twinkle gone from his eyes, and he was suddenly doubting what he was saying.

"What's she like?" I asked.

His head lowered, and he looked pained. "She's one hundred and seventy pounds, *amigo*. How you say it, *fa-a-t?*"

I almost laughed.

Marco added, "But Albert, he *iss* good brother-in-law. She's older too, as old as Albert. His twin sister, ya!" Pain throbbed in his face; but Marco was also trying to put on a brave front, smiling.

I kept looking at him even more, thinking of his loud talking at night. Then imagining that photograph once again; and I was really starting to like him, his spirit, the landscape he was bringing to Canada in a sense, which suddenly began to seem real, Amazonia, my world too. More than a strange memory now maybe. I kept thinking about this for a while.

The next morning I heard Marco leaving the house earlier than usual. Excited he was, and I called out after him: "Where are you heading, Marco?"

"To my girlfriend, to see Marie. She's expecting me. Albert, see—I mustn't disappoint him."

"Really?"

Marco wagged an aggressive finger at me, pointing a few streets away, then marching off.

"Make sure you fall in love first." But my voice was lost in the air, words without effect. *Yes, fall in love first.* My own failed marriage, dismay sometimes eating at my bones. The door suddenly banged shut, the wind coming in full blast.

Winter.

I didn't see Marco again for a while; I thought he was gone, and a vague fear began entering me. And it was unlike him not to say goodbye. The rooming house's fleeting atmosphere: always with dim acquaintances, people you get to know, then never see again. I began thinking it was time I looked for new accommodation; Ottawa was perhaps an elusive place: I didn't belong here. Anxiety gripped me. A letter from Brazil to Marco at the door: from Benedito it said on the envelope. The colourful stamp: a large gaudy macaw, and the address written in Benedito's spidery handwriting, a hurried scrawl.

Marco was indeed around somewhere; he couldn't actually have gone back to Brazil. That night I stayed up late, listening for Marco: the familiar noise, sounds. Wanting it now. All I heard were a couple of winos muttering. Maybe Marco came in late, like a phantom, and left early in the morning. Maybe the Immigration people were indeed after him: and he had to be extra careful; he'd even become suspicious of everyone, including me, wasn't he? A further tremor, somewhere.

Maybe he was now fully under Albert's protection. And still dreaming of becoming a *Canadian citizen* after meeting Marie, no? Or was he now indeed married?

The house remained tranquil for a while, the other tenants seeming to have disappeared. The landlady showed up once or twice. A drunk hiccoughed in his room, as if for eternity.

A week later, I met Marco unexpectedly. He looked pale.

"What's up, Marco?" I asked.

He murmured something; maybe he was trying to avoid me.

But I insisted that we talk.

He cringed. Then he said, "I'm getting tired of all the work, *amigo*. In Brazil, I was an insurance agent. Here, in Canada, I clean rugs all the time!" He sniffed, looking around. He seemed pained as well, face no longer cherubic but drawn. He'd lost a few pounds.

"Maybe when your English improves, you'll get something better," I said. "A better job."

"That's what she too said."

"Who?" I waited.

He sucked in air, making a hissing noise. And I should've guessed— "Marie, Albert's sister. She will be my wife soon," Marco grated. "It's three months since I have been wid a woman." He grinned sheepishly.

"You mean you're not married yet?" I asked, with more curiosity.

"See, I tell Albert to wait a little," Marco added, doubt in his mind, his grimace a strange pain. Pause.

Then he stuttered: "Albert says I no wait longer, or Immigration people will come for me. Remember Benedito, ya? Maybe Albert's right. What you think, *amigo*? Must I really fall in love with her first?" He searched me for an answer.

I became more intrigued.

"Maybe I fall in love with her *after*," he continued emotionally. "That Marie, she never says much. Brazilian woman never like that. But in Canada, now, they become different."

Oddly, I nodded.

"I keep thinking what Marie says, that Brazil *iss* better than Canada. She thinks I should go back there, I have better chance there."

My eyes lit up. "Why did she say that?"

"She says I will always be like other immigrants here, I'll never be happy. Says that all the time. We must go back to Brazil, she and I. But she will only go as my wife. I am confused, *amigo*." He lowered his head, looking more confused.

I kept thinking of his ambition to become a Canadian citizen.

Marco cursed under his breath. "I also came here to forget my first wife," he admitted—for the first time. "She died young. How can I forget her if I go back to Brazil? I really loved Carmen, my wife—so beautiful she was, *amigo*." That photograph, where was it now? Maybe

Albert made him take it down.

"Marie, see, you will love her too," I said on an impulse.

Marco's face suddenly grew pale, as if I'd uttered an anathema.

At that moment Albert walked in, the door slamming shut behind. A surly expression on his face, just as I'd seen the last time. He seemed impatient too, as he said at once, "Hey, Marco, Marie's looking everywhere for you. She's already dressed."

"Dressed?" Marco asked meekly, yet with a raspy voice. He looked really unhappy.

"She's been waiting for you."

"But I'm not . . . ready . . . "

Marco's lips tightened, his entire body tightening.

Albert pretended to look uncomfortable now; he cast a glance at me, then back to Marco as he forced a smile.

Marco muttered, "Maybe I go talk with her first, eh?"—attempting a smile of his own.

"Yes—you better," Albert hissed. "Marie's my sister. No one treats her like that."

"I know," said Marco. "Benedito . . . " I handed him the letter.

I watched them walking out the door, Marco looking more like a prisoner; though he kept up a bold appearance. Albert walking in front, a few steps ahead, leading the way, Brazilians as they were.

"See you when you get back, Marco," I said loudly, and waved. "Don't do anything rash," my impulsive last words, advice.

Marco turned, and waved. I detected a faint smile on his face—that was all.

Waiting, and I kept thinking that maybe before long Marco would return. Alone. Not wanting to go through with the marriage: especially the way he felt about Marie who would return to Brazil. Maybe Marco was really dwelling on thoughts of his beloved Carmen; yet his simultaneous longing, *need*, really complicating matters. Marco and Marie, hand in hand, taking their marriage vows: all expertly arranged by Albert. I imagined there'd be no going back now. Flowers, confetti sprinkled in the air.

Yes, Albert efficiently handling everything, the way he ran the rug business no doubt. I imagined it in further detail.

Now Marco wouldn't be living in the rooming house any more; he'd be gone, to live close to Albert who'd perhaps found an apartment. *For the recently married?*

Or maybe Marco'd be living with Marie's family—with Albert always close by. Now Marco might somehow outwit the immigration people, many eyes being on the lookout for his interest. Yes, his papers would soon be set right, because he was now married . . . to a *Brazilian-Canadian!*

Another letter arrived from Brazil . . . from Benedito? I looked at the envelope, exotic stamps, Benedito there: so quickly he'd been sent back, the plane landing on Brazilian soil; and Benedito, well, he didn't immediately bend down to kiss the hallowed mother-ground of his birth. He only stamped heavily on it, the soldier that he was: an instinctive reaction was all. And maybe after a while he'd talk incessantly, no longer quiet, but assertive, even aggressive: a strange delirium or madness coming over him.

The immense tropical heat, cacophony of bewildering noises, in the streets; a percussion, and more voices everywhere. My constant imagining. Marco walked in, just when I wasn't expecting him.

"Marie's not like my first wife," he quickly said.

"What d'you mean, Marco?"

I looked for signs of agitation. There were none.

"Well, I'm not afraid of immigration people anymore. I am married now, I'm not afraid any longer." He paused. Then:

"But Marie . . . she is fa-a-t!" He said this almost with disgust.

"Albert, well, I hope he will be good brother-in-law," he added. "Now I don't have to work so hard any more. Maybe I won't go back to Brazil."

"But, Marie?"

He didn't answer, but sighed.

I studied his twisted mouth, wide cheeks.

"Come on Marco, you have to face up to it. What about her?" I threw at him.

"It's three months now since I been wid a woman," he muttered, talking to himself it seemed, voice quavering. Then he made a sign of the across, Catholic that he was. *"Amigo,* remember that I think different sometimes, because I'm Brazilian. But I like Canada too—I like it here very much. But I no go back to Brazil. I tell Marie that, I tell Albert too, ya!"

I waited.

He opened Benedito's letter. His face lit up. "Hey, Benedito's coming back. They're allowing him to come back! This is good news, *amigo*. Good news!" he cried. He waved the letter before me, like he was waving a flag.

"Good news!" he sang. "Really good news! Benedito *iss* my bess friend. We play soccer together, we watch films together too, all American—Eddie Murphy, eh. Yes, soccer—Benedito, he play forward!" Pause. "You play too? Maybe we can form a team together." He grinned.

"With Albert?" I asked.

His face took on a strange expression, one I hadn't seen before. Then he ignored me, adding: "I'm not as good as Benedito, you know; I am too fat here." He stabbed at his midriff with mock disdain.

"You will tell him about Marie, won't you?" I suggested.

He looked strange again. "Ah, Marie, maybe she likes him too; likes him better."

I didn't understand.

He cackled a laugh.

"That Albert, he *iss* good brother-in-law. Very good. But Marie, well, she is . . . " He stopped, then, "No, I don't go back to Brazil. I need to send home money, lots of it to my mother, for my child, *amigo*. My mother takes care of Carmelita." He breathed in hard, and as if not knowing what else to say, he added:

"That Benedito. Maybe he will come and go, that's what he's like. Benedito, maybe he will learn to like Marie. Maybe they will go back to Brazil together one day." Again he paused, lowering his head, thinking. Some new truth, something that still puzzled him; that intrigued me.

"That Marie, well," he went on, "she will change. She will start to laugh a lot also."

"What about Benedito?" I looked at him determinedly.

Marco turned away. "He's a *mute*, ya. That's how you say it in English?"

I waited, not sure what to think now.

"Marie'll always be in charge," Marco added. "See, Benedito's really a pussycat, gentle. Maybe he will play soccer all the time. Ya, Benedito an' me, . . . he's mute." He began laughing, and continued talking. Then whispering : "I will remain right here, it's how I feel now in Canada. But not Benedito . . . my *bess frien'* "

Then Marco opened his wallet and showed me a photograph of his child, Carmelita, who had an unmistakeably cherubic face, same as Marco's.

Laughing, Marco was.

When Albert walked in a little later, Marco was still laughing. And all night long Marco would be laughing, I figured—despite Albert hanging around. And I'd keep listening to him from in my room: twisting, turning; even imagining Benedito, who perhaps wasn't really mute . . . the latter returning to Canada because he didn't want to stay in Brazil. Thinking about a plane journey; and a place far away, with real noise, haunting cries of a strange forest, cacophony: more than I would ever hear in Ottawa . . . or anywhere else for that matter because of my own changes: an inner being only.

Calabogie

The two young girls kept throwing the bluish-pink slipper into the shallow neck of the winding lake where the water gurgled, spouted, and occasionally hissed. At this angle from where Laura and I were, the lake seemed more a rivulet, almost dwarfed by the high promontory of a cliff fifty yards to the left, from which divers one after the other catapulted themselves. Below, along the banks on both sides rocks jutted out in serrated formation, some with slippery green moss treacherously carpeting them. To the far right about one hundred yards away, a nude male bather lazily basked on a flat whale of a stone, indifferent to the loud din created by the two slim thirteen-year-old girls; the bather seemed indifferent to us as well.

"Be careful—gosh!" shrieked one of the girls, Jill—long-limbed, bespectacled. The other—Sue—more sprightly and precocious-looking, laughed in the sun, teeth glistening as she commenced a balancing act across the narrow platform rafting the portion of water close to her. Now and again Sue looked at the divers, unreal as they seemed; and perhaps they too were looking at her as she remained poised, her left leg raised, indicating an exquisite curve of thigh tapering to the instep. The afternoon sun glinted everywhere, not least on the cliff divers with an aura of peace; only the playful cries from the two girls shattered the quiet, the bespectacled one directing the other to the slipper as it tugged against a large rock. From time to time the girls glanced at the nude bather, who seemed in his early twenties, their shrieks becoming more insistent. The entire spot no longer appeared covert or the monopoly of the one bather; now it echoed with a benign hostility as the girls shrieked louder. The nude bather, as far as we could tell, shifted from his reclining position and looked more studiedly at the girls trying to retrieve the slipper. Suddenly the girls seemed tense.

Laura, lying next to me on her side, a white-spotted greenish bikini with a tongue of strap poised on her navel, blonde hair spangled in strands reaching to her ribs, also looked at the slipper as the current pulled against the rock. The girls seemed even more tense as the slipper now remained stationary. Laura muttered that it needed nudging before it could get into the running stream again. The shapely body of the one precocious girl, Sue, became steadily arched, poised; but Jill, with agitation, kept on urging her to get on with it: to reach out and grab the slipper!

Laura lifted her shoulder, neck, to get a better view. I did the same, leaning closer to her, while the nude bather appeared to stand up, then sit down again, still as pumice in the August sun with a shimmer and haze everywhere. The cliff divers again catapulted themselves into the unfathomable depths, as if lost forever.

A delicate wrist reached forward, almost pulsing in the sunlight. "Go on, get it!" cried Jill, the bespectacled girl. But the slipper was held by the resinous moss, evading the outstretched hand; and just when it was on the verge of breaking free, it seemed held again by a tangle of moss about to distil the slipper's pink-and-blue coloration. A further surge of water, the current pulling in one direction, the slipper with a tail of moss in another.

"She won't get it," Laura said, breaking into a dim smile.

"Maybe," I replied.

"No."

"She will." Oddly, I stiffened.

The nude bather rose, sat down again, smiling in the sun, his body outline now more than a silhouette, well formed as he was; and he seemed now less indifferent to us, no longer in a world of his own. Laura looked away from him to the slipper and the girls, the hand still stretched out, fingers like tendrils reaching further. My attention shifted to Laura, her well-shaped back, taut muscles curving close to the lower spine and glazing in the sun. "She won't get it," Laura repeated, urgency in her voice.

Jill rubbed at her glasses, then shrieked like a seagull that was lost and was now finding its way back with others. The other girl, Sue, rangier now, kept leaning forward as far as she could, her entire body stretching, about to touch the slipper.

At this odd moment I decided to playfully caress Laura's shoulder, vaguely wondering why we decided to come here at Calabogie outside of Ottawa; Laura had suggested this spot, I recalled. "It'd be private," she said, on our first real date. Maybe she wanted us to really get to know each other: we'd talk about things we didn't previously say despite a vague shyness, discomfort in her. Now with the two girls vying to get the elusive slipper, the discomfort somehow seemed accentuated. Once more came the intrusive sound of the divers, thwarting our expectations in a way; another diver, screaming as he floated in the air, then finally hitting the water. The next, a woman in her early twenties, hefty-looking in her silhouetted form, lifted her arms, body taut in the sun, and soon after dove in!

"You know, it's amazing how they do it," Laura muttered.

"Yes," I said, following the diver's plunge, as if considering my own vicarious leap.

"They're good at it too." Laura added, turning to my side, an almost questioning look in her eyes. "I mean, those two." She pointed to the thirteen-year-olds still trying to retrieve the slipper: their determination now above all else; and the nude bather fidgeted as far as I could tell, no longer comfortable being part of stone, rock, or landscape ahead. But my attention was quickly rivetted again to the slipper, the water tugging harder, the moss itself pulling it no doubt. Jill, determined, took her turn now, grit etching her mouth, her eyes seeming smaller behind the glasses as she tentatively moved forward, stepping upon the next rock, and the next. "I am scared," she blurted out, freckles iridescent behind the grey glasses.

"You mustn't be, Jill," encouraged Sue, turning in the direction of the whale of stone, the nude bather like pumice still in the distance.

"I can't help it!"

"Gosh!" came the punctuated reply.

Laura chuckled and seemed more attractive as I contemplated her: it was all part of her manner in this seeming wilderness with more rocks, trees, the weather perfect, lulling us further. The next diver on the cliff, a strong, wiry-looking youth with curly hair: a gymnast as he seemed, spinning in the air before hitting the water with an almost reluctant splash. Just then I heard the one girl closer to us crying out, "Get my slipper. It's mine!

"I can't," answered Jill. "It's too far away!"

"You must; it's your turn!"

"I am trying; but I'm scared!"

The moss, as if in the air; the next diver, circling in the water. The nude bather, still basking, slowly getting up.

"It was you who threw it in!"

"No, you!"

"You did, deliberately."

"No!"

Their caterwauling, defying me to drowse; then, like incantation: "Get my slipper!"

"I can't!"

"GET IT!"

Suddenly, loud-pitched raucous laughter: the precocious one glancing in the distance to the nude's silhouetted form, her hair thrown back, mouth, lips pursed. Jill, as if always bespectacled, raged on:

"It was you! You can't deny it; you threw it in, Sue!"

They argued, laughed, then again began stepping onto more slippery rock and moss and moving with the current, filaments of grass. My eyes closed, dreaming in a way; the nude bather looming larger, shifting with the clouds close to the divers.

"Don't deny it!" one girl shrieked.

Laura merely watched me, and smiled, caught up as she was in the girls' playful jibes, frenzy.

Opening my eyes, I looked into the water: at how black it suddenly was with a dim movement. Shadows, the clouds drifting, darkening. A further amorphousness not far from the girls' feet against a ledge of stone, moss, as I started thinking how earlier Laura and I had glided along the water; and I was reluctant to enter, but then suddenly cartwheeled into it, being unable to maintain my grip. Laura thoroughly laughed. Soon after I swam behind amidst eddying whorls, her long hair golden against her skin's tapestry as we gradually moved closer to where the cliff-divers kept coming in like suicidal lemmings. An hour of floating, paddling: my own selfconsciousness in a way, as we sometimes hailed the divers from afar, excited "strangers" as we all were held in a common bond by the trees, rocks: all our silent moments, reverie, then intermittent splash. Another diver coming in; and just then we looked up in dread, awe.

I figured Laura was now thinking about her ex-husband, Perry: he, in Saint John with their two-year-old Meaghan: the latter spending the summer with him. Laura was absolutely devoted to Meaghan, thinking about her daughter's safety all the time. And what did Meaghan talk about with her father? About whom Laura was now seeing?

"It's your fault!"

"No . . . yours!"

"The slipper, you must get it! It's mine!" clamoured Sue.

"No, mine!" hooted Jill, like an echo.

My eyes were now glued to one spot in the water close to us where the two thirteen-year-olds stood and then frantically waved. More amorphousness, something moving, clambering with invisible, yet palpable arms; a distinct shape. Laura, silent, as if she'd now drifted away from me: was no longer by my side in the seemingly wayward sun. Then she stirred; she too was looking fixedly at the one spot. *Had she seen it?*

*

Almost three in the afternoon, it was, but now time seemed strangely irrelevant; nothing else mattered in the consistency of weather, like glue; the world itself now indecipherable with water, stone, sky, the lake's widening perimeter. The nudist standing up in the angle of sun, his expression one of strange intensity. A crow floating above, skirting the trees, branches, the air whirring; the slipper quickly moving sideways. Sue's wrist throbbing as she once more leaned forward: it'd be her last attempt, her hand shaking as she concentrated harder. Jill urged: "Go on, you will get it now!"

There were no snakes here, I thought; the rock formation, the crevices, holes in the ground, underwater. Something still moving . . . NO! A prehistoric semblance, or elongated form that once was a part of stone carpeting the moss: with eyes, mouth, teeth, a distinct head. It kept moving towards Sue with a deliberate intent; her wrist still throbbing.

I turned to Laura, who was smiling, her own impenetrable guise maybe, and still thinking about Meaghan, wasn't she? The watery object seemed blended with the environment, akin to a diorama, unreal. An odd rhythm, too, the object moving slowly towards the outstretched hand.

I rubbed my eyes, harder.

The girl's hand pulled back in an instant, as water gurgled.

"It's so amazing," muttered Laura with a tranquil ease.

"What is?"

"The kids—what they can do. What they're up to. Their parents perhaps, diving maybe. When I was their age, I wasn't ever allowed to be alone." She yawned.

I concentrated on the moving object, eyes, teeth; moss, greenish-yellowish. Both girls now looking directly at the nude one as he started walking towards them in the afternoon air. Instinctively they blushed, one bashfully lowering her head. More determined were the nudist's strides—he was bent on proclaiming the area as his own. Another crow hiccoughed and moved blackly against the disc of sun, swirling in the direction where the divers were, the lake mirroring the cliff as if with a distant eye; the horizon itself seeming to move forward. Yet I kept studying the formation—like an obsession—searching for a clue to explain it as it appeared removed from all else: the sky, divers, depths far below. *Another diver coming in!*

The snake, or whatever it was, seemed to derive from the moss— things unseen—palpable, creeping out of rock and sediment, gliding forward: but it really wasn't.

The one girl's outstretched hand, Sue's delicate fingers, wrist; my throat dry. Laura stiffened. She saw it too!

I searched the reptile for a mouth, flap of ears, a semblance of what it really was, and wasn't; other appendages; gills; a tongue whipping out. Laura, her body still tense, threw a look at me: an odd questioning expression. In a further angle of sun, another diver loomed, face an odd, twisted grotesquerie as he began to somersault before finally landing in the water with unexpected precision.

"You alright?" Laura asked.

I didn't answer. But I kept looking at her, as if she was the one who wasn't alright. And why were we indeed here? How well would we get to know each other? The nude bather was now walking deliberately towards us, and one of the girls let out a wild whoop, as if in total disarray—Sue, with long curly hair, her cries shrill amidst the birds' somersaults, the sun's wild glitter and haze. More divers coming in all at once, as if in a further collective drowning. And that snake—still curling and uncurling in the water, making a commotion really. *Let's run away,* I heard: a mute tongue's expression.

"Come on, Jill!" called the other.

"Let's first get the slipper, Sue!"

"It's too late. It's not mine!"

"You said it was yours!"

The nude one kept resolutely coming forward, the sun itself now felt like a slab of rock upon us. And Jill started crying, sobbing. And Sue, well, she lamented—looking at us as if for help, as the bather kept on coming; then Sue started sobbing. And the current surged at their feet, and they bent down at once as if their lives depended on it, on all of the lake, water; on the nude bather not coming any closer.

Laura instinctively stretched out a hand towards me, managing a smile; but now we were both looking at the nude bather, hoping he would stop . . . maybe he was just an illusion of the sun and sky, or a distinct shadow. Maybe. My eyes fell upon the water again, but the girls' melodramatic cries, sobs, seemed to frighten off whatever it was: which was no longer there! That object, serpentine in a way amidst the rock, moss, was now translucent. Lurking . . . the nude bather advancing.

"Come on, let's hurry!" cried Sue, in mock desperation.

"Yes, we must!"

"No, let's stay some more; that slipper!"

"We must hurry!"

"What for?" Sue's accusing, harsh eyes. "I can't run barefooted!"

"Yes-you-can!"

Laura desultorily muttered: "Children nowadays, they're a far cry from when I was growing up." She'd said this before, even as she looked at the nude bather quietly claiming his spot, his territory in a way, from the deliberate strides he took in the unabashed air.

Laura added: "You see, it's for real. Maybe it's just fun these days.

Life for them is, I mean." Wistful she looked, and maybe she was again thinking of Meaghan. "Soon, they will grow out of it, maybe."

*

I once more looked into the water, at every bit of flotsam, moss, weed; and I imagined a hand reaching out, a frail wrist; fingers' tremors; the slipper itself close by. The nude bather a hundred yards from us: he'd paced himself well, and he stopped, tentative, not sure what to do next, hovering there. The two girls suddenly started to run away, hopping across rocks, stones. It was all they could do it seemed. Then Sue turned around, as if to have a last look at the nude figure: no other, nothing else; and she screamed hard once more, and then sobbed . . . because of fear of a sexual attack?

In no time both girls were sprinting fully ahead, leaping like fauns, constantly urging each other on, *to hurry up!*

I watched them ascend the cliff amidst bramble, rhododendron, sage brush: to be with their parents, sisters, brothers—all the divers. Laura watched them too, as if expecting another collective dive, a daring somersault in the air. It was the two girls' turn now maybe. The air rose about us. A *swoosh*. Laura, well, she held her breath. The nude one, standing there, also looking at the girls high up, about fifty yards away; maybe they could all see us better now—see everything better as they lifted their arms, then started to flutter, ready to fly, slim bodies etched against a bland sky. Breasts, hips, thighs, waist; I waited for the familiar shrieks, a primal scream—whatever—before they hurled themselves down.

The air kept them still; the sound or silence, a mute voice; the girls still flying in a way, bodies floating in the gauze of sun, the eddying current below; the nude bather, astride a rock, steadfast; crows' wayward ascent. Applause from the others . . . *down, down*. I looked into the vortex of the pool. I waited for the girls to surface; Laura's hand in mine, fingers tightening.

Why then I began looking again for the amorphous form, I don't know. I thought I saw it: moss, with eyes, teeth, mouth; an appendage, ears, a chest that curved, underbelly: a stomach propped against a small ledge of rock; a tail swishing with hairlike ends. Laura's hand still in mine, tightening . . . Would they ever surface—those two? I kept thinking of the lake swallowing them forever. No! I imagined their wet faces, and so lovely they looked while leaping off the cliff . . . And where was the slipper? The nude bather, close by . . . he was now retrieving it with a strong hand, fingers pointed; he also kept glancing sideways at the cliff, then into the water . . . and maybe he'd lift the slipper in the air like a trophy just when the girls surfaced, diaphanously, clad with ringlets of water . . . out of foam no less!

I remembered just then Laura and I in the water earlier, her gold-spangled body, hair: so lovely she looked, really attractive. And why was I with her and no other? Our uncommon origins, our difference: she white, and I—markedly different, with distinctly brown complexion. Our longing and expectation amidst trees, rocks, here in this semiwilderness spot we also thought was ours!

"We should be getting back now," Laura muttered. "It's getting late."

Our hands intertwined, with a vague tension, surprise and yet expectancy. Will they ever rise up—those two, remaining so interminably long at the bottom?

I began to imagine Laura and I now climbing up to the cliff: and our future lives depended on it, our hands tightly held, clutched. Next we were diving off, sailing in air: our mammoth breath; eyes looking down to the very centre—the far bottom—where moss subsisted on moss; stone on stone. And right then I saw the two girls, hair streaming against their faces at the far bottom; arms and legs working; lungs pumping at full capacity; eyes closed, cheeks puffed!

But I was really on hard ground, Laura still next to me. Instinctively I looked again for the nude bather with the slipper in his hand.

But he was no longer there; he seemed to have vanished in the sun. And I imagined the girls rising up in a swoosh, their heads puncturing the formidably placid surface of the lake. And those left on the cliff, the adults, all started rhapsodically applauding; it was as if they were really applauding us—Laura and me. Jill and Sue were also applauding; as if in a way telling us that their game with the slipper was just for us; no other. Our fate being tied to it!

Louder, the sounds: against the crows' formation in the far sky. The sun too coming down into the water. And above, below, the thing unseen, yet seen. An object no less, more palpable, in the mind or imagination, swirling or slithering, and yet being fully at rest.

Homecoming

Her first night in the tropics: with him; and she hadn't slept much; mosquitoes seemed to be buzzing all night long. Maybe in the early hours she'd fallen into a deep REM sleep, come to think of it. Fully awake now, Sheban was determined to enjoy her stay with Frank: in this distant place, many rivers, mountains crossed. Frank, of course, was born here, and she'd be married to him one day soon, she hoped. The early-morning cock-crowing sounds amid noises of people filled her with a strange excitement.

Frank stirred. "Slept well?" he drawled, pressing his body against hers, then kissing her lightly.

The gauze of white net around them, which Frank's mother had fashioned: now twisted at the edges, furled, almost intertwining them. She kept studying it. Further voices . . . downstairs, and a loud cackle of laughter. A dog barking. Frank got up, stretching; now indeed Canada seemed so far away. Sheban getting up also, with a sudden anxiety, and together they started walking down the stairs in the solid wooden house built on stilts. Frank wasn't his usual confident self: he dithered, smiling awkwardly as he was about to face his family; his mother mainly—he was meeting her in full daylight after almost five years. Frank had once said that in the tropics time seemed eternal; and maybe so much had changed between him and his family: he, the eldest "child," and still his mother's favourite, no? Maybe Frank had acquired new habits, customs, in Canada, hadn't he? And would there be concern about he and Sheban having slept in the same bed because they weren't yet married—this being an affront to his mother's sensibility? The old giving way to new, Frank hoped, told her, laughing. Sheban also hoped.

He took her hand at the bottom of the stairs, thinking: night's arabesque, the atmosphere almost overwhelming. "You'll have a good look at my mother now," he muttered. "It was dark last night when we came in, remember?" Sheban suddenly began feeling strangely grateful to be here.

Frank's mother greeted them at the foot of the stairs: the old woman's instinct about things, her narrow cheekbones, eyes dark pools literally, as she looked at Sheban . . . her future daughter-in-law? Frank had said that after his father died about ten years ago, his mother was left to run the family's affairs. He'd regaled Sheban with stories about his mother's inner strength, despite how frail she looked.

"I'm glad you come home, son," the old woman said. And to Sheban, "You slept well?" Sheban forced a smile.

"I'm glad to be home too," Frank repeated what he'd said last night, curtsying a little.

Sheban remembered studying the old woman's face in a photograph Frank had once shown her: the strong lines, angularity of jaw, chin. Now Sheban casually mentioned the mosquitoes; she was expected to say this perhaps.

"They don't have mosquitoes in Canada?" the old woman grated, not without some annoyance.

"Well, er . . . not in the winter."

Frank scoffed. "Oh, they have lots, in the summer; bigger ones than here, Ma. In the forests."

"Forests?"

The landscape, many regions, provinces that Canada was. Tundra, fir, pine, numerous lakes, rivers: Frank talking, prattling on, laughing. The many races of people too in Canada, didn't she know? Sheban was thinking she'd taken Canada for granted: she'd grown up in Belleville, Ontario. Others: nieces, nephews, now listening in, a few neighbours also, such a crowd all eager to see Frank and to "look at her." Sheban was self-conscious.

Tell them about your Irish ancestry, Frank had urged. Oh?

Sheban kept hoping she'd go to Ireland one day to meet her forebears.

Frank's mother, Rajdai, offering her guests the morning's special fare: fried ochro, shrimp, which Sheban really liked. The spices were hot, aromatic. Everyone watching them as they ate hungrily.

The old woman muttered, "You shoulda come home earlier."

Sheban looked across the table at her.

Frank grinned.

The old woman's face grew solemn. The other relatives clustered closer.

Sheban parrying further questions, while Frank jiggled his eyes, teasing in a way, urging *her* to tell all. The old woman continuing to assess her, *them*. Suddenly Sheban wanted to be alone with Frank: it was what she had in mind for a holiday, didn't she? Being in the sun, the full tropical splendour, and she hoped to return to Canada with a really good tan! Frank looking at her, smiling. Sheban concentrated on her food . . . and why did he really bring her here? *To show her off?*

"Yes, you shoulda come home earlier," Frank's mother whirred.

They sped off in the family car: to visit friends, relatives; and it was as if the entire village, district, was one large family. Frank being his old self, chippy, gregarious; the air tinged with smells of zinnia, frangipani, all that he breathed in. She breathed in. More smiling faces, and everyone kept adoring her, followed by invitations for more food, drink. The car stopped, with further exclamations: "It's Frank and his *wife!*" "No, his girlfriend. She's beautiful! She's . . . *white!*" Laughter, all their genuine admiration.

Sheban figured she was starting to get used to them. The pulse of the sun's rays, yet the trip was beginning to feel exhausting: she was starting to get tired. But Frank said with a further sweep of his hand, "Meet more of my friends, Sheban. Come on, you must!"

Amidst the relatives' further solicitations, he added to her: "I haven't seen them in seven years, my entire family." He chortled. He called her Sheba, his pet name for her, roguishly smiling. "Inhale the trade wind too, it'll invigorate you, Sheba," he crowed.

But hotter it was getting, and she didn't think it would be this hectic, suddenly.

The flat coastland they travelled, passing other cars, draycarts, people sometimes dawdling, hailing them again, all instantly recognizing Frank talking about the last relative, Mohan: his infectious ways,

"Mohan too wanted to come to Canada once. But he's decided to remain here. Maybe it's because he married Indrani, his childhood sweetheart," Frank added. "How I wish I was here for it! Mohan has never forgiven me for being absent, you know, he and I being childhood friends."

"You never told me that before, Frank."

Houses on stilts seeming to cartwheel; palm trees rolling, wavering. Sheban blurted out: "Your mother, she thinks you belong here."

"Does she?" Frank concentrated on his driving, as they passed more houses, shacks. Here where Frank was born and raised: it being so idyllic . . . so far from Lake Ontario now. And her early memories of Belleville close to Kingston, Lake Ontario, the happy childhood she'd had. "Why did you ever leave, Frank?" she asked, looking at him as he gripped the steering wheel. He quickly tried to avoid hitting a cow that had veered onto the road.

"After my father died . . . " he began. Then, "Oh, do I have to go over that?"

"Yes, Frank," she said, equally testily.

"For God's sake, Sheba, what's the matter with you?"

"Nothing's the matter with me."

Frank swerved, the car screeching to avoid hitting a donkey that stepped in the middle of the road.

"Christ, we don't have to quarrel. Not here I mean," he said.

"Is it because of your mother?" Sheban wasn't sure why she asked that.

"It's the heat, the excitement too, darling," he murmured, then leant and kissed her on the cheek.

But Frank's mother would soon ask about whom they'd visited, and what she thought about each relative, wouldn't she? This moment, now, when they arrived home again.

Frank said to his mother, "I'm beginning to feel I've never left here, Ma."

His mother smiled, pleased to hear this.

Frank: "I should've remained behind, like Mohan." Impulsively he embraced his mother, taking her by surprise.

Sheban looking at the old woman as the latter muttered to her son: "If you hadn't gone to Canada, you wouldn't have met . . . "

"Oh, Ma!"

Sheban simply forced a smile; as the other woman looked at her.

The next day: the beach; all that Sheban longed for, wanted in a holiday: the allure of ochreous sand, stretches of palm and coconut trees, waves hurling across the wide sweep of the coastline bordering the Atlantic. This was going to be it now, for them to enjoy themselves, she and Frank. The splashing, wading, then swimming in the water, with other relatives inevitably joining them. Kingfishers and seagulls skirting the air, swooping down next to snatch tiny mullet or mackerel. Sheban inhaling the trade wind fully . . . and two, three, four days quickly going by, her being away from Frank's mother and some of the tiresome relatives; and she was starting to become more acquainted with Frank's real friends, despite their discreet stares at her.

Frank still happy, smiling, despite moments of his temper, impatience because of the humidity no doubt. Now boyish he looked in the ocean, the foamy waves reaching up to him . . . and to Sheban stripped to her barest. Frank teased her about being daring: here in the openness, the Aphrodite of the sea as she was! Laughed. Yes, let them see how unabashed she was: with none of the false modesty of the local women. They were all smiling, laughing. Frank laughing loudest, as Sheban pulled at her bikini straps. "Let's see how far you can swim out, Sheba," he called out to her above the sound of breakers.

Rhapsodic voices, the combination of wind and waves: and so playful she'd become as the waves lifted her high, buffeting her in the hurl and sweep of ocean. The others applauding, encouraging her to go out farther. Frank standing about twenty yards away, more dark-hued in the sun he seemed, watching Sheban with a wide grin on his face "You're marvellous, Sheba!" he yelled above the surf and the seagulls' raucous cries. The salt sprays whipping against her eyes, nostrils, tingling her as she kept on laughing, then swimming out to the edge of the world almost. And there was no thought of Canada, of her job in Toronto, now . . . *of ever going back.*

Frank coming after her, hands reaching out, brushing against her waist, thighs, closer. Those on the beach applauding. Frank, looking back at them: joyful spectators . . . marvelling at him and Sheban. After a while they rested on the beach, with choice green coconuts out before them; and hungrily they drank the tasty coconut water, some dripping down their necks, arms. The coconut jelly: gosh, it was delicious; Sheban smacking her lips, as more was offered to her, which she gulped. Laughing. Hair wet, ringlets about her ears, neck. He said he'd been doing this nearly every day when he lived here: this familiar past-time with Mohan and the others . . . and why did he ever leave here?

Impulsively he leant forward and kissed her. The others applauded. And in the dilation of her eyes, the way her skin seemed flushed, Frank figured she was now indeed happy, crystal sprays of salt water dried on her torso, thighs, her entire slim body. *Let them look at her!* Sheban suddenly wished she had a towel close by. Her sense of modesty, bashfulness, maybe, as Frank noticed behind the shell of a coconut as he drank.

Sheban also drank, quickly, throat a distinct lump as she clasped her legs, thighs together, modesty instinctive now. One relative said it was time to start fishing with the seine: they'd soon eat fresh crabs, shrimp, all that the ocean offered, beneficence, a veritable cornucopia. Everyone quickly took up the challenge; and Sheban was once more excited.

Frank held one end of a large seine close to her as they waded into the water, *teaching* her how to go about it. "It's fun," she cried above the breakers, the trade wind again hurling salt sprays like mild whiplash. Sheban hitching up her bikini against the undulation of her waist as she held the other end of the long, wide seine. Frank, grinning, telling her to be careful since the waves could easily steal her clothing away. The others' ears perked up. "It's been known to happen," Frank hollered. "In fact I've seen it!" "Seen what?" Sheban yelled, stumbling against a wave.

"A woman's bikini pulled away, just like that." Frank laughed hard, like a schoolboy.

"You're making it up, Frank," she hurled at him, hair falling away from her eyes.

"Yeah, it's true—it happened to an American woman; gosh, she was beautiful!" More laughter. Manoeuvring the seine close to the neck of the beach, with more waves hurling. Suddenly Sheban fell, a boisterous wave pulling her forward. Frank quickly let go of the seine, dashing after her, but Sheban started swimming ahead. Frank took after her, the surf swirling as he tried encircling her waist, tumbling forward. Kissing her passionately next he was, as never before. And in a way she wanted this to happen, though she instinctively fought to free herself. Grabbing Frank's neck she was, pulling him against a choir of waves singing in her ears. Louder the others' applause, as her eyes took in the wide expanse of sky, clouds tumbling down into the ocean, in this tumultuous moment.

Under the mosquito net that night Sheban whispered, "You know, you shouldn't have kissed me like that before them. You said that . . . well, they aren't used to such show of emotion in public."

Frank made a playfully muffled sound against her ear. "They aren't backward you know."

"But?"

"Oh, they're used to it," he said nonchalantly, nibbling her ear.

She playfully fought him off, because her thoughts again drifted to his mother: "What about her?"

But Frank was busily burying his face into her thick brown hair and breathing in perfume at the back of her neck, ears, his ardour, passion rising. Hers also. Their words meshed with the night, as everything else seemed no longer important: only a strange pulsation, further arabesque, their intertwining bodies. "I love you, Sheba," he cooed. The ocean's pulse in the night, the tides' own, coming and going. Mosquitoes buzzing afar, or close by. Their breathing harder and recreating the sea in moonlight; the friends, relatives, all their hilarity in the night's turnaround, the bed—with an old bamboo frame—creaking loudly. Softly.

Still nestled in each other's arms they were, as she said, "Eager to return to Canada?"

"You?"

"I asked first."

Yawning, she turned away, refusing to think about it. The night's hum, like distant stars in their lives, closer. In a way, she was lucky to have someone like Frank in love with her, she thought. And when he figured she'd fallen asleep, he heard her sniffling, crying.

"What's the matter, Sheba?" he asked, leaning across her.

"Nothing."

The smell of her hair, musk. Her fragrance. He waited.

"It's, well, because I've never been so happy before in my life," she said. And . . . "

He kept thinking.

"I missed so much of the past . . . in your life I mean. Maybe . . ."

"Maybe what?"

She dried her eyes, "It's because I had such a wonderful time today. Your relatives, friends, they're such wonderful people." She nestled against him.

Frank looking up at the ceiling in the dark; the night hovering it seemed, as he started wondering what it would have been like to have grown up in Belleville, Canada.

Sheban added, "You know, it's your mother I want most to please."

"Nonsense," he replied.

The whirl of their individual thoughts, as they also tried to fall asleep during a lull. Mosquitoes yet buzzing outside the net: the palpable tropics. Their conjuring up further images, and yet trying to fall asleep. And the next morning they'd both be tired, they knew. Fidgety. The stream of sunlight, night and day somehow inextricably linked, becoming one. A constant dream world also, transitoriness. Ochreous beach, wind and waves recreated, amidst further arabesques, despite the morning's light.

"You both look pale," said Frank's mother, greeting them when they came down the stairs.

She was laying the table, the pasty curried shrimp: she'd risen early to prepare it. Flat bread, chapatis, with such an aroma, which they yearned for.

"Maybe you been too much out in the sun," the old woman murmured, her way of scolding. Looking at Sheban, demanding to know why she couldn't have been more modest on the beach. The unmistakable allusion, word had gotten back to her.

Frank glanced across the table at Sheban. "I guess so," he answered, humouring his mother.

"Maybe in Canada it diff'rent," Rajdai added, a distinct tremor in her veins. Sheban's thoughts whirring, as she ate. The old woman looking at her steadily, firmly.

"Oh, mother, it's all the same. Here, there—it doesn't really matter." Frank's casual banter, generalizing their behaviour, still lighthearted.

"People will talk," the old woman grated.

"Let them," Frank brushed her off, his Canadian way now. "Besides Sheba wasn't naked, she had on her bikini."

The old woman cast a quick glance at Sheban. "And you, what do you think?" The voice still firm, uncompromising.

Sheban felt cornered.

"Maybe you'd be glad to go back to Canada soon, no?" The old woman dithered as she pulled at the plate before her, her lips, entire jaw dropping.

"We don't have a choice," Sheban managed. "Holidays do come to an end. Too quickly," She looked away.

Frank, sensing the tension between them, put an arm around his mother, clucking his tongue in an almost idiotic way. He added: "I will come back again, sooner this time, Ma. It won't be five years again."

And maybe this was it, this length of time that he'd been away from his mother and the imminence of his leaving again, so soon . . . making his mother edgy.

"You've said so before," the old woman hissed.

"I promise this time."

Eyes on Sheban; and the old woman's voice droned, "Maybe you'll only come back when I'm dead!"

"Dead? You'll live a long time yet, Ma. Maybe up to a hundred." He laughed.

"No," the old woman cried.

"Yes," as if he was becoming impatient with her.

They ate quickly, all three. And where were the other relatives? Maybe the old woman orchestrated things in such a way: she wanted them to herself. Sheban's and the old woman's eyes met again.

She no longer had an appetite, Sheban felt. Yet Frank ate ravenously, and from time to time he looked at the women and forced a smile.

"What are you going to do today?" Rajdai asked after an embarrassing silence.

Frank muttered, "I'm tired of the beach. Maybe we'll take it easy today. We will stay home with you."

But Sheban had already focused her mind on the beach, the freedom she'd had: which she'd never felt before, not even in Canada . . . or Mexico or Europe where she'd been. The waves, wind's song in her ears, surf along the shore, the seagulls, kingfishers; the horizon canting with the vista of clouds and skies. So magnificent it all was, breathtaking! She was looking forward to it again.

"Maybe we'll start packing. A day and a half more, then we will be going back to Canada," Frank muttered, searching for justification of their impending return.

"Packing?" the old woman rasped. She stopped eating. "But . . . ?"

"We have to leave, Ma," Frank offered, like a palliative.

Rajdai looked hard at them, eyes widening, a rush of air coming out of her mouth, as she said: "Ah, it got to be. But . . . but you're not my son any more!"

"*Not your son*? I am, Ma!" Frank reprimanded, in a fashion.

His mother quaked with silence, her head lowered, as if permanently.

That day went by quickly, without much happening. More relatives, they too were aware the holidays were coming to an end. And one or two kept asking about Canada, the unique place it was . . . and one seemed curious about the Eskimos living there, no? Frank still cheerful, despite the fact that his mother had grown sullen and kept dabbing her eyes with a silk orhni to stem the tears.

The last day of their stay, Frank embraced his mother, cooing, "I will return again, Ma. I promise, soon." And no doubt he meant it. Sheban watched him, considering the affection between mother and son. "Just wait an' see, Ma," Frank emphasized, as the old woman remained lachrymose, self-pitying.

Then, "Don't mind me, son," she replied, drying her eyes.

Frank aware of the old woman's eyes on Sheban—the latter talking to some other relatives now and promising to write to each one, scores of letters.

The old woman added, "Maybe she's the right girl fo' you, son. See how well she's getting on with them. If you been married to one like us, it wouldn't be like this." Her almost cryptic words, but Frank knew exactly what she meant despite the air of disingenuousness.

"I love Sheba, Ma," he managed a reply.

"Maybe this Canadian girl, she likes it here. Just look at her, and them around her." It was as if the old woman was talking to herself; then she chortled, surprising him. "See how she makes them happy, even giddy by what she's telling them."

"Sheba likes it here. The beach . . . " he droned.

"The beach?" hissed the old woman. She waited, inhaling hard before adding, "Maybe I'm old now, near seventy, an' the world changing. It's the young people—their turn now." She fought the self-pity welling up in her.

"You come back, both of you," she added haltingly. "Yes, I want you to come back here before I die!" she muttered in a muffled voice, which seemed all.

Toronto's high concrete buildings on Bay street, the business capital: here in this large city with its endless run of races, people of all shades, description. Frank and Sheban reliving their holiday with images, photographs: the overwhelming scenery. The ocean's pulse, too; other aromas lingering; and to friends in the office, Sheban showed the photographs again. Frank did the same in his irrepressible way, though he also mulled, contemplated: a new side to him, some said, akin to prolonged daydreaming. Longer days becoming weeks, months.

Frank woke up one morning and said, "I'm going home."

"Home?" asked Sheban.

"I belong there, with them."

"But what about . . . me?" An instant tremor in her.

He waited.

"Us, Frank?"

He wasn't sure how to tell her that his mother, well, was ailing; and maybe she wouldn't live more than two or three months. Finally he forced the words out, telling her his true feelings for his mother. And would Sheban come with him? The ocean, all that she loved, wanted—remember? Of course he'd be making a sacrifice to return there, his job, future . . . and she, if she came, it'd be the same. A whirl of images, tangled emotion. "You know I love you, Sheba." Maybe he should stop calling her that. She conjured up the old woman's wrinkled face, eyes, the relatives all around paying her a special respect, solicitude, including the sometimes jaunty and irreverent Mohan.

"Frank, must you really go?" Sheban moaned, and looked accusingly at him.

"I've been thinking about it, more and more." Like a confession, his words, and his studying the way she was taking it.

"Oh?" She stared at him.

"You really could come with me," he repeated the offer, as if he somehow knew she wouldn't agree; it was too much to ask of her.

"But?" was all she could say—a retort, complaint amidst her pain and a mild frenzy. And inevitably she kept thinking about the old woman who perhaps was now more crotchety, fussing about everything, including her imminent dying. But maybe she'd live on, longer than anyone of them. Maybe. And inevitably, the beach, ocean, ubiquitous palm trees, eaucalyptus shrub; that day, she remembered, when they'd eaten delectable coconut jelly. *How could she ever forget!* Looking at him and still wondering what she'd actually do there if she returned with him. It couldn't simply be whiling time away on the beach. Besides, she'd have to depend on him, his family. Her mind's whir, immediate disarray.

Just then Sheban felt she didn't know Frank any more, a gulf between them, widening . . . over these past few months, as if their two years together really meant nothing.

"Canada isn't really my home," he managed.

"Isn't it?"

"No, Sheba."

"But it is," she argued.

He muttered about living a lonely life in Canada, in the cold, snow, winter in Toronto. This image: his juxtaposition of it with luxuriant rice fields and being with his family, other relatives; the scent of rotten vegetation and mud with its own special aroma which he was familiar with as a child: hard work, their farming life once lucrative (could be again). Mohan, jocularly saying to him after an hour working in the humidity, "You see, Frank, it really's hot now. It not like being in snow and ice!"

Mocking laughter, Mohan's sometimes sly, ironic way.

Frank also laughing, vicariously wiping a ring of sweat from his brow. Next he was thinking of the family investing in a tractor: which they'd always wanted, to avoid the drudgery of manual work. Mohan smiling, telling him that one day they'd even be exporting rice to Canada!

Sheban, murmuring to herself: how she'd be alone for a while; maybe after he left she'd start dating again, perhaps. Life's fleeting relationships: ah, she couldn't simply wait for Frank to come to his senses. Her mother, friends, all telling her that; her father urging her to find one of her own kind. *Oh Dad!*

Frank opened the letter with the Canadian stamp on it: familiar it was, and Sheban's handwriting, confessing that she thought about him all the time. And how was he doing? His reply, the words forming, his wanting to know if she was now going out with someone after nearly six months of his being away . . . *how much he missed her!* His mother, still crotchety, looking over his shoulder, sensing the letter's contents.

"Is that girl, no?"

He nodded. Irritable all of a sudden; and was it because it'd been another hot day, and he was finding it more difficult to cope being back home?

He didn't often sleep well now because of the humidity: his twisting and turning endlessly; a million mosquitoes in his room it seemed, too. Heavy rain falling, drumming on the zinc roof, the incessant rhythm. Suddenly he felt he was in a strange world, not the familiar tropical place where he was born. Thinking of snow falling in Canada, too: the streets wet, slippery, cars skidding; yet it was peaceful, comparatively quiet, the whiteness of snow being all.

Again reading Sheban's letter, he was; as he also stirred after a short spell of sleep or lull of consciousness. Sheban's words indeed in his mind, and maybe she too was wake, despite the expanse of ocean, waves; then the mudflat, somewhere . . . they were together on it, crabs scuttling about, here on the edge of the world: in a strange no-man's land. Barefooted too they were, as crabs scuttled around them, running out of holes with the rain now pouring: as he lunged at the next crab with a sharp knife, a sickle, going after another . . . until they had an entire boatful. Oh, the fun she too was having, and the expectation of roasting small crabs over a slow fire . . . what a delightful taste it'd be!

His eyes wide open . . . perspiring . . . and he wondered why he hadn't gone to the beach again since returning. His mother saying to him, "It late, son. You got to get up earlier. Rice planting cannot wait, or else the sun go dry it all up." Pause, then: "Mohan said you don't belong here any more."

Frank didn't answer, he was tired. His mother continued on about Mohan's mocking comments, as well as all that was now passing through the other relatives' minds about him.

He turned away from her; but she stood there, expecting him to reply.

"I am returning to Canada," he said.

"Mohan said you would." Her voice flat, almost inaudible.

"He did?" He was immediately angry with Mohan and with all the other relatives; even with his mother, that look on her face.

She nodded. "When?"

"Maybe next week," his voice abjectly weak.

A moment of silence, then his mother, not without self-pity, said: "I'll soon be dead, Frank."

"Don't start that again."

He stood close to her, muttering what he felt compelled to say: "I love her, I love Sheba. Maybe she misses me as much as I miss her."

"Go, if you must."

He went to the rice field that day, though he felt like staying home and brooding even more: Sheban perhaps now in her office, writing a memo or report, which she did quite frequently as an up-and-coming manager.

Mohan working close to Frank, and muttering: "When you go back, Frank, tell them how hard we work here; that it isn't all fun an' games—the tropical paradise they think it is!" Voice grating, yet determined, no longer smiling.

"Tell them working in the rice field is not like office work in Bay Street," Mohan rasped. "There where people hardly sweat; and you'll tell your children that too, when that times comes. You must, Frank!"

Mohan, working tirelessly, bending down to cut the rice stalk, so swift his action was, a tuft of rice held up, then shaking the grains in the air, like a trophy.

Frank watched his rhythm, movement: Mohan bending down once more, and mud spattered about his face in the swamp. "Yes, tell them all, Frank," urged Mohan, gulping in air. *Maybe* . . . and now Frank was really feeling the hot sun bearing down on him.

"I will return, to come and see you again, Mohan," Frank answered, to the wind, with a mild shriek in the air, among the leaves; his voice fading, while Mohan kept on working and talking, berating:

"This is no pen and paper work, Frank; no computer work with soft hands an' wearing collar and tie, see!"

More wind tempering the heat, the cool air really; and Canada, Frank yearned for just then, especially Toronto . . . and Sheban waiting for him at the Pearson International Airport, no? No other! Amid a thousand others, all returning from somewhere, including new immigrants, refugees to be with their hosts, friends, relatives, welcoming them with so much excitement. Strangely Frank felt he was the only one different, this feeling gripping him, here at the airport. And lonely he felt. Where was Sheban? Why wasn't she here to greet him?

Panicking. A knot forming in his throat. A pulverizing fear, too. The feeling of being in no-man's-land: this time in the cold and ice, with stormy weather blustering outside. He was suddenly frightened as never before; and his mind started coming up with all sorts of reasons, excuses . . . Sheban perhaps coming home late from the office and not being able to make it to the airport on time. Maybe. The reality of the present . . . who he was, still wretchedly alone. The feeling almost nauseating. Then he heard her voice: "Gosh, Frank, I was held up in the traffic, you know. The winter driving conditions!"

"You were?" he rasped back, then quickly moved towards her. And so pleased he was to see her, as they embraced. And he wanted to tell her that the tropical sea was still singing in his ears, the entire ocean, and she was beside him; looking at her, determinedly, smiling. The strong wind now blowing against the car, the windows, and the grind of the highway traffic in the bitter cold.

Black Jesus: A Fable

West Indians are wanderers . . .

COLIN MACINNES

I.

The nickname "Cyclops" came to him, like a strange baptism; and his holier-than-thou Aunt Mabel, when she heard it, quickly became animated: and it didn't matter if she had just walked out of the Holy Gospel Fundamental Church of God itself waving a hymn book—she cried out to everyone to stop calling her nephew by such a name. "Stop it at once," she clamoured, beating her breast. "See, he isn't like de rest o' you!"—as if anyone needed to be told that. Mabel's white mantilla almost dislodged from her head, she kept on at it. Yet, *Cyclops:* it was funny how the Greek word sounded to her ears; confusing, baffling. Then overnight the name seemed to change to *One-Eye,* like a miracle.

"One-Eye's for real," others hooted, and Mabel seemed able to stomach this new name—she was never heard to complain again. And One-Eye, lanky, gaunt, kept walking around by himself; being in a world of his own, some said. Mabel shook her head, wondering what would eventually become of him; and she looked at his one bad eye, and kept thinking about One-Eye's parents leaving their only child to be in her care. *What for?* Looking at One-Eye again, intensely, Mabel swore there was an insect there. "A moth?" asked the fellas, ready with ridicule; and the left eye seemed strange, the more everyone looked at it—like a curse.

Now fellas started putting a hand over their own eyes—looking left, then right—pretending they were blind; some squinted hard. "Impossible!" they cried; and one shuddered, saying the island sun itself was making him blind, as he started calling himself Samson, flexing his muscles and pretending to push the walls of his house down. "Look at me!"

he cried, stumbling forward, still blind. And in church once more, Mabel continued singing out allelujahs, thinking that what One-Eye lacked in sight he made up for in height. There was no thought now in her mind of a malfunctioning of his glands, because everyone was supposed to be born perfect: such were God's holy ways. *"Amen!"* Mabel rang out again; and other voices loudly chorused, "Allelujah!"—as if mimicking her.

Outside the church Mabel, with her white mantilla on, muttered, "He's a blessed child, you will see," which caused more frowns. Then, sucking in air she announced that she was planning a party, *a going-away party*. One-Eye was walking around and sporting a fancy wool suit in the hot sun—he seemed indeed preparing for his going away. Fellas quickly gathered round him, asking, *Where are you going, One-Eye?*

"To the land of colleges and universities, to Canada," he grated, with guile, though solemn.

"Hey, One-Eye, you t'ink you could cope?" they ridiculed again.

One-Eye lifted his head high, pretending to be not amused.

"You's only nineteen, an' that place so cold, man. An' why d'you really want to leave your God-fearin' Aunt Mabel behind for?" They kept baiting him, and One-Eye pulled at his lapels, imagining he was shivering in the temperate cold. *Oh?* Then booze, food, at the party. *Freeness in the air!* Mabel, infected by the mood all around, smiled widely and watched the fellas swallowing rum-punch in large quantities. One loudly guffawed, then cried out like a revelation: "That One-Eye, is too much brains he got!"

"Yeah, with the same dead eye—shrivelled like old newspaper," answered another.

"Not closed, like a coffin?"

"In Canada maybe he'll work miracles. One-Eye will indeed make the blind see."

"Just like that?"

"Yes, just like that."

"Praise the *Lawd!*" Mabel answered.

Then they started playing dominoes, a game charging their spirits with excitement: which gave their lives meaning, all agreed; and One-Eye, strange too as it was, began turning out to be the best damned player around! With the one dead eye, he also seemed to be a clairvoyant, as he kept on winning. "One-Eye playing dominoes the way fellas in some countries play chess—so deep is his concentration," hailed another.

"Yeah, he could be our own Boris Spassky!"

One-Eye concentrated harder on his dominoes, and there was silence all around.

Another whispered, "Look at he good, that eye, winking sort of. It's a thinking eye, by Jove!"

"Amen!" Mabel let out again.

At the Piarco International Airport the plane's engine revving up, then whirred loudly—a sound so overwhelming, the like One-Eye had never heard before. *Hurry, One-Eye, you late!*

One-Eye started hiccoughing, and his now distraught Aunt Mabel began crying because her "boy" was leaving her for good; and only when One-Eye stopped hiccoughing did she dry her eyes, but she kept on moaning. Then One-Eye began muttering gibberish, and fellas swore it was because his aunt had pumped so much religion into him that it was now all coming out—he was speaking in tongues!

The plane rose in the air, and One-Eye imagined he was flying in the fabled bird of paradise, now taking him to Canada where he'd be living among millions of white people. This thought gripped him more and more, frightening him a little. Right then he wanted to return to the island: to the place where he was born, just as Herbie Collister (known as Guppy the Fish), imagined would happen: as he kept muttering to Mabel still at the airport waving to him.

But One-Eye was suddenly feeling trapped in the plane; while the Fish kept telling Mabel that when One-Eye actually returned home, he'd bring genuine change to the island of Tobago. *Crusoe's own special place!*

"Amen," repeated Mabel.

Fish, sometimes a sceptic, kept telling Mabel about promises local politicians were making everywhere in the Caribbean; more garrulous he became—berating the local politicians because nothing they promised ever came true! But when One-Eye returned to "the people," the island would become a place of real paradise, just as it was meant to be.

"Amen," muttered Mabel.

Fish gritted his teeth as he looked up, and maybe he was thinking of the going-away party once again, and the dominoes clapping loudly. Yes, let the politicians beware.

Higher up, the plane's engines still whirring, and One-Eye began to feel he was *going closer to see the face of God!* Clouds forming all around, and he suddenly started praying, as a new vision filled his mind—new sensations as he'd never experienced before. And, indeed, the strangeness of the place called Canada with tall concrete buildings entered his mind's eye: all in a new land, a new heaven on earth!

II.

For a while, One-Eye was glad he'd left the island. And so amazed he was at what he saw, all around him, that he kept moving his head left and right, continually.

Walking about the streets of Toronto, he began seeing fellas in fancy ties and jackets made of silk, like zoot, some pretending to be top-class dudes. *Ah, seeing was indeed believing.* With his dead eye, the eyelashes flitting, One-Eye quickly looked the other way—wanting to avoid his own kind. He concentrated only on people from different parts of the world; and on Dundas Street where he occupied a room, he took to listing the names of all the countries people in Canada said they came from, until he ran out of ways of spelling these names—especially places in Eastern Europe and Asia. Before long, he'd filled an entire notebook. Next, he looked up these countries on a map and tried pronouncing the names one by one, thinking he'd figured out a sure way of getting an education. He carefully considered the Italians, Lebanese, Greeks, Portuguese, Bosnians; next he imagined showing his Aunt Mabel this notebook one day when he returned, and started laughing by himself. "Amen," he heard from somewhere. And maybe he was still flying in the huge bird of paradise, with wings flapping, the engines whirring in his ears.

Then he stopped writing letters home, even to his Aunt Mabel, or to the Fish, or even to Big-Bonnet Stella whom his aunt had wanted him to become betrothed to. Then snow started falling, and One-Eye's fingers, ears, suddenly began to freeze—so cold it was becoming . . . his teeth chattered. One day, he remained huddled in a corner on Yonge and Bloor streets, his coat collar pulled up, and One-Eye began blaming his aunt for sending him into this God-forsaken wilderness . . . Canada!

He started going to strange places in the heart of winter, like a true wanderer. He'd take the subway, then the tramcar: and sometimes he ended up at the Bramalea City Centre. Now he saw dudes, with their women, some doing strange or ungodly things in public all the time listening to loud music on gargantuan ghettoblasters. Yeah, if his Aunt Mabel knew about these things, she'd quickly want to haul his tail back home. Her cry still in his ears . . . and such was his own pain and suffering, he felt.

A fella wearing a long earring on the left ear came up to him and deliberately peered at One-Eye, as if he were some kind of a freak. "Man's you's a pirate?"

"Eh?" One-Eye grunted.

"Women would find you kinky, brother, with one eye an' all," charmed the other. "Say, would you like to do a thing or two for us?"

One-Eye didn't like the drooling look on the cat's face. "What kind o' thing?"

"You could dance nude for a start, I mean. Tall as you are, the women—"

"Eh?

"They'll think you're hot chocolate, man!"

One-Eye recalled his Sunday school days at the Holy Gospel Fundamental Church of God, and how he'd sing out allelujahs at his Aunt Mabel's prompting—a real God-blessing time as it was. Now he was being tempted to do the *wickedest* things possible, the very same the Minister had always warned his congregation about—things done only in Sodom and Gomorrah!

"Come on brother," further charmed the fella, patting his face.

One-Eye wasted no more time—but fled!

Now he kept going to the Jane-Finch area, as if pulled by a magnet: to Chalkey's Bar. Rasta fellas with dreadlocks hanging about their ears, drinking Red Stripe beer and muttering the name *Jah Rastafari*, seemed to be everywhere. One-Eye watched them playing dominoes always huddling close to a white fella named Krapps. The latter, mean-looking, hardly ever smiled, as he continued winning.

One-Eye's eyes widened, because he'd never before seen so much money being passed around from the many black and brown hands to the sultry Krapps.

Closer he drew.

Krapps immediately sensed something in the air; he became uneasy. He turned and looked at One-Eye. And some said it was from then on they saw Krapps become nervous, which was why he quickly challenged One-Eye to a game.

On that first occasion One-Eye won, incredible as it was. And everyone started appraising One-Eye, wondering where he'd come from, how long he'd been in the country. *Was he illegal or a refugee?*

One-Eye merely concentrated on his game, and Krapps grunted again—as One-Eye once more won.

Now fellas from all races (many from places One-Eye hadn't yet copied down) watched Krapps play intensely against One-Eye, a real tournament as it was becoming: which some of the neighbourhood newspapers run by Jamaicans gave coverage to. One columnist boasted that One-Eye was a true, bona fide Jamaican adding to the multicultural mix of Toronto—never mind the police-shooting of black people, or the one wearing a beret calling himself an immigration consultant and yet being accused of rape!

More rasta fellas came and watched the game between Krapps and One-Eye, intensely; and maybe they forgot about Jah-Rastafari for a while; as they were all genuinely amazed that One-Eye could win so easily against Krapps. From the many islands, all sorts of small, obscure places that they came from—some boasting about their two-bit Caribbean island as if it were bigger than China itself! Indeed, they kept watching One-Eye in deep concentration. Then one said he knew One-Eye from *back home*, and he was a genius since then! They followed One-Eye's moves, like a shadow; some even imitating his mannerism.

"That man can see wid the dead eye open. It like an insect in there waiting to crawl out!"

Another laughed, muttering that One-Eye was starting his old habit of seeing things which no one else could see. *Clairvoyant that he was.* One-

Eye turned around and looked at this one, not saying a word.

"Play on, One-Eye," let out an impatient Krapps. "Let's see how good you are!" Krapps was losing his cool.

One-Eye played, and matched perfectly with his *sixes*. Again he won! Everyone applauded, some declaring that a black man winning over a white showed the black race's superior intelligence.

Slowly One-Eye hauled away his winnings, like manna from heaven; and it was the only time they said they saw him smile—such a sweet smile it was, as if he was receiving blessings from God.

"Man, you should head for Las Vegas," growled Krapps under his breath to One-Eye, acknowledging defeat; he watched One-Eye slowly count his winnings—and decided never to play with him again.

Others hollered, sounding the clarion call: "Who dares challenge One-Eye? Black or white! Religious or non-religious!" No one came forth . . . and One-Eye was left alone for a while to mutter, chant, or simply concentrate . . . *on what?* No one knew exactly.

Fellas said One-Eye was thinking only of his Aunt Mabel, especially with another winter on the way. And maybe he was disappointed with life in Canada, and was thinking of doing something about it.

"Come back home, One-Eye! You belong here. You, the genius and the true saviour of the Caribbean people!" cried the Fish—like the fabled Robberman, from afar: he'd heard the news of One-Eye's victory over Krapps.

"Nope," One-Eye said to himself, shaking his head like a dog or horse wagging its tail.

Another asked, "Is what really cause you' eye to go bad, One-Eye?" And: "Can you really see with one dead eye, *mon?*"

But One-Eye merely continued shaking his head; and they left him alone in Chalkey's Bar, in a corner, to reflect now on the names of all the countries he'd copied down, which he also repeated to himself and he kept thinking about the state of the world. But others figured that winning all that money from playing dominoes—he'd become different, *stranger.*

"What will One-Eye come up with next?" asked Chalkey, watching him slyly from behind his counter. "That man's brains does hatch fire!"

"Amen!" came affirmation.

But others argued that One-Eye indeed wanted to be alone: he was in a form of retreat right here, like being in a desert or on a mountain. *Yeah, like a prophet—a real John de Baptist!*
"AMEN!"

III.

Head held straight up, and looking taller—and in an almost grand manner—One-Eye announced that he was starting a new religion. Neck stretched to its fullest, he proclaimed: "This new religion is for non-believers and believers alike to save our black brotherhood from eternal damnation!"

"No shit?" fellas at Chalkey's Bar reacted, some with a look of awe.

But One-Eye said no more: not for a while. He merely kept on contemplating, pondering the nature of the universe and all things that mankind believed in; he reflected on wars, ethnic group against ethnic group, tribe against tribe. And he moaned.

"It's God's ways in action," others hummed, thinking this new religion might catch on like wildfire, if One-Eye really set his mind to it. The Rasta fellas whirred, hummed, dreadlocks hanging, wavering. "Yeah, One Eye's now saying he could make the blind see!" intoned another, himself like a prophet, though, admittedly, a false one.

"Holy Jeez!" others hissed incredulously.

"Is One-Eye really our Black Jesus then?" cried Chalkey himself.

"Like a second coming?"someone else put in, sounding puzzled.

And thereafter in Toronto wherever fellas gathered, in all the bars and clubs the talk continued about this new religion, including in places in North York, East York, Scarborough, Mississauga, everywhere else—always about this strange one called One-Eye, the best damned domino-player around, to boot!

Those standing on Yonge Street close to *Zanzibar*, the strip club, asked, "Is it really true?"

"What's true?" asked a gaudy blonde nearby, looking like a butterfly.

"Yeah. Our own One-Eye could make the blind see!" cried an instant believer. "The *See-Through Religion* will save your soul, woman!"

The blonde moaned, beating her chest, suddenly, like a medieval flagellant; then, she cackled a quick laugh. But others chorused that it was starting to happen: the blind beginning to see because of the power of God invested in One-Eye and the *See-Through Religion!*

More imposing-looking and sporting a full-fledged beard, One-Eye next stood before Eaton Centre in the heart of downtown Toronto on Saturday night, and harangued about his new religion. The crowd slowly started to swell, though many came out of curiosity to hear One-Eye rant and rave and swing his arms about. New faces, new converts, including a few tourists: some merely wanting to see black people making fools of themselves (it was whispered).

"Amen! Amen!" came spontaneous incantation.

One-Eye raised his voice to further proclaim the *See-Through Religion,* which would save all mankind from the wars and rumours of wars! It was also a religion, One-Eye added, that would save the environment: the entire ecological system going sour as seen in drastic changes in the weather. The *See-Through Religion* was against the arms race itself, and against dividing all other races too. The microphone whirring, One-Eye kept up the harangue; and no one knew where he got the equipment from: it was as if Eaton Centre itself was behind him, in a bid to attract new customers. *Never mind the dope-pushers!*

Back in his apartment, One-Eye put on a headset and kept listening to his favourite rap music, while still thinking of making the blind see. Mrs Goldstein, the old woman who lived alone in the apartment below—who'd always wanted to go to the Caribbean but could never afford to—smiled by herself: she kept hearing One-Eye walking up and down, the music still beating.

When she finished making her best apple pie, she knocked on his door, and offered it to him. One-Eye grinned from ear to ear, realizing he was very hungry.

Then Mrs Goldstein watched him click his fingers, his eyes closed, the headset still on as he tasted the pie. Next One-Eye started swaying his head, still feeling the beat; and she suddenly felt she knew One-Eye really well, and *genuinely loved him*!

In the street again, fellas asked, "Is it true what you're telling us, One-Eye?" They were all his potential converts, weren't they?

"It's the blessed truth which will make you free," One-Eye intoned. His lanky frame seemed lankier, his voice stirring them with rhapsody; his elocution like that of a true Broadway actor (as he sometimes fancied himself to be): "Seeing is believing, brethren," he cried.

Then snapping his fingers, *click-click*, reggae beat in his ears, he started doing a fancy footwork to match the Bob Marley rhythm. This immediately caused the white cats nearby to become enthralled. *It's cool, man!*

One-Eye clamoured, "It's the only true religion—the very word of God!"

An inspired brother let out loudly the accompaniment, "Amen!"

Another hissed, "He will soon make us believe such an impossible thing as a camel going through the eye of a needle!"

One-Eye twisted his body skinny as an eel, as inspiration kept seizing him, with distant echoes of his Aunt Mabel's *Allelujah!* in his ears. He continued exhorting his believers not to waste time any longer . . . but to truly seek the Kingdom of God.

BELIEVE! he cried.

A believer said to his fellow brethren, "This Brother will want us to keep away from white people born-again pentecostal religion."

"Isn't he Malcolm X reincarnated? Next he'll be talking about the evil society white people created around them."

"Is he like Elijah Mohammed too?" asked another.

"He's not a Muslim—black or white," countered someone else, a former Hindu hanging out on Gerard Street like a fixture—who also was a believer.

Others immediately saw the practicality of the new religion because of its multicultural vision . . . all here in Canada . . . as he cried: "No, shit. It's what we need in Toronto to make our people truly celebrate. It will no longer be complaining about cops shooting us all the time!"

"Yes, black identity is all. Religious affirmative action. And it's our own God-given path to salvation!"

But from a stodgy Jamaican intellectual wearing thick horn-rimmed glasses, the reply: "The *See-Through Religion* will bring ridicule to the black race. It's not like Caribana, which is the *freedom* from slavery that our people are still celebrating!"

He was quickly hooted down, because others were in favour of this real prophet from the Caribbean—predicted by Marcus Garvey, Dr Dubois, and others, no? Such was the emotional state now among the *black brethren*, everywhere; even rapso artists and dub poets were proclaiming him on stage.

When One-Eye appeared before Eaton Centre again, more than one hundred people showed up, all wanting to see him "in person," they said. In a flowing white robe and looking distinguished, One-Eye arrived and commenced preaching; and he inspired "his" crowd with his particular black mystique, it was said. Quickly they began chanting his name, praising the new religion.

"Tonight's the night for the first real witness of the *See-Through Religion*," One-Eye proclaimed. "You will see and believe, one and all!"

Believers and non-believers alike became tense—as excitement and anticipation rose in the air.

One-Eye raised his head, a stork ready to swallow innocent fish swimming in the waters of a river called Babylon. He began calling out . . . for someone to appear from the crowd, someone afflicted with blindness. *Come forth . . . Come forth!* He looked up, heavenward, dramatic as he was, invoking the power of the Almighty God, and again calling for someone to come forth . . . *the first real witness!*

"*COME FORTH, COME FORTH!*" he cried, beating his breast.

Mrs Goldstein suddenly stepped out from the crowd, and she seemed blind as a bat, stumbling forward.

"Heal! Heal!" cried One-Eye, rushing up to her. Then he whispered something in her ears, almost embracing her: such was his inspiration and affection.

Everyone was breathless with anticipation.

Then Mrs Goldstein opened her eyes wide as moons, and smiled. One-Eye, half-blind as he himself was, quickly held up her hands for all to see.

Awestruck—all were.

"Behold, brethren, this woman, who was once blind—can now see. Seeing is indeed believing!" Sucking in air to catch his breath, he added: "She's a witness of this same *See-Through Religion* I've been telling you about. Behold, O Mighty God on High, it's a miracle."

"Amen!" chorused believers all around, which included the former rastamen who'd watched him play dominoes against the redoubtable Krapps.

But sceptics rushed to Mrs Goldstein and asked, "Is it really true you can now see?"

Mrs Goldstein nodded and croaked, "All with the power of the Lord."

"How did he do it?" asked a giddy-eyed cub reporter from the *Toronto Sun* assigned to cover the ethnic community.

"Ask him, he's the prophet," she snapped, pointing to One-Eye. "I am Jewish, don't you know."

"D'you you believe in Christ, Mrs Goldstein?"

"I've always believed in Christ," she retorted, the excitement suddenly being too much for her. "Jesus was a Jew . . ."

"What about the Holocaust?"

She opened her eyes widely at the questioner. "What about it?" Then she added that the truly blind were those who had eyes and yet didn't see!

And to One-Eye the fellas added, "This is a helluva thing; this gonna cause headlines all over the blessed Caribbean. Wait until your Aunt Mabel finds out about it."

But One-Eye now wanted nothing to do with the Caribbean. He stood aloof, pointing to Mrs Goldstein, his skinny body gyrating, twisting sexily, as the women noticed.

One-Eye on TV next: with jacket and tie on—same as he used to wear on the island—standing before a microphone and still haranguing about his exotic *See-Through Religion* which was inspired by the true God of the Universe. This image gripped his listeners' minds the more he talked: and all watched him; in particular they watched the insect-laden eye, how it quivered, moved as he talked. The camera close up, focusing on the dead eye all the time.

His hands raised, invoking the power of God. And his charisma was everything, better than those on *100 Huntley Street*, all agreed.

Then One-Eye started telling everyone—all of North America—that as a child he had the misfortune to lose his left eye in an accident in the erstwhile Garden of Eden (the Caribbean)—the same that fell from grace with all sorts of corrupt politicians calling themselves leaders of the people. Now God's only ways were true revealing and healing ways!

A further chorus of voices rose, in every corner of the great city of black brotherhood and sisterhood, Toronto—the everlasting meeting place for all the races of mankind!

IV.

One-Eye returned to Chalkey's Bar, hoping to see the forlorn Krapps, the former East German communist; and he wanted to convert Krapps to his *See-Through Religion*, with fellas now a-buzz with excitement. One-Eye grew solemn, an air of sanctity about him. Chalkey whispered, "One-Eye's meditating. No one should disturb the contemplatin' of the Word of God."

"Allelujah."

Silence for a while, longer, then One-Eye muttered, "The truth shall make you free," still talking to himself; then he focused his full attention on Krapps and the others playing dominoes.

Quietly he got up and gathered all the money from Krapps's table, deliberately counting the twenty dollar bills; and none could stop him, such was his mastery, his poise, as if all the money belonged to him in the first place.

"One-Eye's up to something," Chalkey added, watching him.

"He is?"

Krapps started smiling, like a giddy child.

"You sure, brother?" someone asked Krapps, as if he'd indeed become a convert to the *See-Through Religion*.

One-Eye's lips moving, as he started muttering: "Whereupon a man cometh from the sugar bush, therefore must the same man return and be singing hallelujahs on a donkey's back." His eyes closed, he hummed a mantra, a benediction: all in one. Hands still held out; and it didn't matter if what he was saying was sheer gibberish.

Krapps, like a troubled soul, quickly began putting more dollar bills into One-Eye's hands. Other fellas also began emptying their pockets, in a new expression of belief and love.

One-Eye added: "Poor an' black as you are, yeah, you shall receive the more you give. *GIVE* . . . brethren! You can only find salvation through me . . . to ease all the drug-taking—the ganja, an' crack an' cocaine destroying your souls. I am the Prophet with one eye who indeed can make you really see the evil before you." Then One-Eye closed his eyes and lapsed into deep meditation again.

Chalkey whirred, "Leave him alone."

"Yes," said Krapps," leave the power of God alone."

For days after, the fellas argued about One-Eye's special appeal, and about the particular wisdom of his words—all his profound truths. They also said domino-players everywhere were innately authentic believers, which was repeated by Krapps . . . a disciple now intent on following in the footsteps of this black prophet from the Island of Paradise known by many other names: Patmos, Atlantis, El Dorado, Barbados, Tobago, Grenada.

A really blind man in the street started muttering, aping One-Eye— saying how indeed a Black Prophet will be the saviour of all the races of mankind. *Yes, he would!*

"Believe, believe!" cried the truly blind. "You have eyes, yet you do not see!"

"Amen," cried others, in utter disbelief.

Ubiquitous as he now was, One-Eye appeared in people's living rooms all across the city (some said across the country); and on Vision TV no less, he kept spreading the word of God. Suddenly it was like a thousand dominoes falling one after another, and nothing could stop it; and the precursor of this religion was a man of Jewish faith, no less— none other than Brother Henry Kissinger who, without knowing it, had proclaimed about all Latin America and Southeast Asia the famous "domino theory" now accepted in the White House of America as gospel. Praise be to God! "Praise the everlasting hand and creed of politics that will bring about liberation," another cried.

Mrs Goldstein also began talking about an affinity between the *See-Through Religion* and the Torah. But an irate Hasidic scholar angrily countered, "He's a false prophet!"

One-Eye's picture appeared in the front page of the *Toronto Star* next, a feature article tracing the history of black people in the Caribbean: these same people who were the most God-fearin' in the western hemisphere, all because of their experience with slavery not so long ago; the same who'd practised voodoo in dark hovels and worshipped the goddess Erzulie in their longing to ease the pain of long suffering. And all the descendants of the former slaves were now indeed living here in Canada . . . inhabiting the Great White North!

Further pledges of money came pouring in support of black pride and sympathy for all oppressed peoples everywhere in the Third World—all because of the momentum of the *See-Through Religion*. Ah, One-Eye had done the strategically astute thing of mentioning the Jewish faith as an influence, hadn't he? Some Caribana organizers—erstwhile protesters against the reopening of the musical *Showboat*—had growled at this.

And in whatever hall or basement One-Eye went to, more money was thrown into his hands. Later, counting all the money in his apartment, One-Eye snapped his fingers, reflexively. And Mrs Goldstein, below, heard him, and kept hearing island waves: her vacation indeed, finally.

Before Eaton Centre the next Saturday night, One-Eye knelt down, wet and snowing as it was, and prayed, thanking God for small mercies. The "congregation" did the same, and more donations, pledges, poured in. One-Eye prayed louder, and some weren't sure if it was a tape-recorder they were listening to now, or One-Eye's true voice.

"Amen!" came a rhapsody.

All eyes still closed, so strong was their devotion.

About fifteen minutes later, when they opened their eyes again, then saw no sign of One-Eye. He'd disappeared.

Snow starting to fall heavily in this land of temperate heaven . . . and One-Eye's disappearance was itself like a miracle. The converts closed their eyes again, praying louder, thinking that when they opened their eyes once more—One-Eye would suddenly reappear.

He didn't.

Krapps, looking gaunt, as if he hadn't eaten for days—akin to a Lazarus-figure—muttered to himself in Chalkey's Bar that maybe One-Eye had gone to Las Vegas, the inveterate gambler that he always was.

"What?" came a shriek from the truly blind.

Krapps nodded.

"Impossible!"

"Where else d'you think he's gone then?" Krapps burst out laughing, like a mad man: as if he'd known all along about One-Eye, which none of them ever suspected.

It was Mrs Goldstein who really confirmed that One-Eye had indeed gone to Las Vegas; as she wiped away the tears falling from her "seeing" eyes. And maybe she'd been planning to go with him, hadn't she?

It took converts—the ones who'd pledged the most—two full weeks to make up their minds to go after One-Eye in Las Vegas. This way they planned to recover their money, all agreed.

Finally the "delegation" found him lying dishevelled and drunk in an alleyway called Spit's Alley, with no money in his pocket.

"All gone," One-Eye, defeated and drunken-looking, said; a pitiable sight he was, no less—and barely audible. He opened his one good eye and looked at his brethren, now his accusers, his arms raised, as if in readiness to be nailed to a cross as atonement for his wrongs.

"It's de way of sin," he droned, making his confession, "which a man wid only one eye couldn't see clearly." He hiccoughed, then opened his eyes widely, challenging them to accuse him further.

"So, you see, brethren, I will remain here in the wilderness of America, in this only true Garden of Eden. Praise be to God," he cried.

Moans all around.

One-Eye kept talking, his voice one of pure lamentation; and the follower who'd said he knew One-Eye from back home on the island slowly handed him a letter from his Aunt Mabel.

One-Eye reached out, nervous, fingers fluttering—as he recognized his aunt's crisp handwriting. Slowly he began reading: "Dear Bobo . . ." He stopped—and closed his eyes, and lowering his head like a man forever doomed. Then he started praying, those around him also closing their eyes.

Somewhere the sound of a plane droning, far above: the sounds coming from the same island he'd left forever . . . and from where he'd first seen God's shining light amidst a dark lining of clouds. And One-Eye wanted to tell his accusers about this now: this vision, in his most plaintive voice . . . while still seeking their forgiveness.

The plane droned louder, and One-Eye started crying like an infant; and there was nothing else his accusers could do or say to him, they realized.

Returning to Toronto, the "delegation" quietly reported that One-Eye couldn't be found. They were sure, though, he'd never be seen in Canada again; or even on the island of his birth (Tobago) because his Aunt Mabel had now publicly condemned him: denying his very existence on the radio and TV, even blaming his parents for leaving their only child in her care. *What for?* In the Holy Gospel Fundamental Church of God, once more her voice rose, less loudly, "Allelujah!"—and plaintively.

Drive Me Until I Sweat

It is winter again and really cold, and snow's falling everywhere; and maybe soon it will become a blizzard. It is at such times that I think about a place where the sun shines all year round, and where it's warm and beautiful: like where I've come from. Don't get me wrong, it's not bad being here in the Big Apple. And, believe me, here one can expect things to happen, miraculously, sort of. Yes, like getting rich by saving all one's hard-earned cash, though it's only by driving a cab. So I mutter to myself, *Harvey-boy, money breeds money, if you know what I mean—if you could handle you'self properly.* And my thoughts are again filled with sending money home to Barbados, and with the island exchange—as I've been telling Esther these past years—I will return home and retire to live like a king (or queen, as Esther'd quickly remind me about herself).

Yes, Esther—God-fearing as she is an' all—says she'll never come here to New York City to live with me, though the phone regularly rings and she's making sure all is well with me, here in New York. Laugh all you want when you hear what I'm about to tell you. And I'm saying to Esther I'm doing my best driving taxi, and I will return home next year, or the year after! She says I'm obsessed with making the *holy million!* That God and Mammon—the mighty twain—shall never meet. But I say, America is America—there's no place like it; and I'm determined to make my million, driving taxi night an' day, and on weekends too—and in good weather and bad weather and in all other sorts of weather too, if you catch my drift. I imagine greenbacks floating up before me across my windshield, cold as it is now, with the snow still falling; and sweet Jesus, it's like a dream coming through the more I think about it.

Yeah!

The wind's starting to blow harder, the streets becoming slushy, so difficult it is in this February month now. And fellas outside, I see, are freezing: I can tell. I tightly roll up the windows of my cab, and start feeling comfortable, turning to drive round Manhattan . . . going onto Fifth Avenue once more. And some of them I see hailing me to stop are from the islands—it's not hard to tell—and I'm wondering what they're doing up here in this blizzard, 'cause they're not bona fide Americans. Yeah, maybe some of these same fellas are muggers, pimps, layabouts, holding up their collar close to their ears—as they look—and I smile to myself, and still hear them swear loudly at this God-awful weather. *Esther, d'you hear me!*

Cruising along Wall Street, I take my time, cause it's no use hurrying with the wind steadily picking up, blowing flurries so that I can hardly see where I'm going. More bone-chilling gusts; and glad I am to be in my *yellah bird*—and I'm yet thinking 'bout the *holy million*; and that time will come when I will indeed return home, *Esther!* Then I won't be thinking of attending evening classes at City College with dreams of becoming a lawyer one day, you hear. Though I admit such ambitions have been with me a long-long time now, since I used to live in Barbados. And maybe it's for such a reason Esther'd decided to marry me ten years ago, cause she'd seen a future in me! Yeah, I could make it big once I get into the *professions*, as Esther calls it (she's always dreaming the wonderful dream for me). But sometimes, I say, how can a man be driving taxi night an' day and hope to concentrate on books?

Going over a pile of snow, I crawl through at the traffic lights at the next intersection, with the wind rising to another flurry. Now it's beginning to feel like the worst winter New York will ever have; and maybe nowhere up north in Canada it's like this now—it being such an accursed time of the year.

Accursed?

I better be careful with my words, so Esther doesn't know what I'm really thinking. But let me give it to you straight about life as a cab driver. Yeah, I don't like picking up black people, cause a man can't get rich that way; so I'm choosin' my customers carefully in America the free! Yeah, when a despatcher isn't bothering me, I pick up white people only, cause they're the ones who will give me the biggest tips: the same ones I see coming out of large offices every day, attache cases in their hands and many wearing fancy suits, men and women alike, and they look so confident, always on top of the world.

So I'm still choosing my route carefully, and it's Wall Street again, as I watch folks in large winter coats, some looking like secret service agents too . . . so what's money to them, I say! They can afford to be generous with a fella like me, a bona fide islander intent on rising from rags to riches. Like Horatio Alger, no? See, Esther, a man sometimes has to be practical about things: he has to be a survivor, cause here it's not like Kingston or Bridgetown where a man can saunter down the street and dream about nothing in particular an' still feel good about himself.

But here in America, it's different—and it's the *holy million* that you need to feel really good about, which keeps occupying my mind more and more, no matter what the weather's like. See, Esther, that day will soon come, and I will say: *Look, woman, see with your eyes, the sweat of all these years, now that I've made it. Now let me see a wide grin on your face to tell me that you're happy!* And Esther's eyes will pop out when I show her the hundred-dollar bills, all greenbacks like manna from heaven. Now she and I can indeed live comfortably, and not worry about a thing ever again!

I imagine Esther smiling, muttering in her fashion, then protesting, *What's the point now—we're too old to enjoy it, Harve!*

But I quickly tell her that if I'd remain on the island I'd still be a stevedore, porter or janitor, with rheumatism an' arthritis eating at my bones. So, you see, in America driving taxi is tiring work, but a man can be his own boss inside his *yellah bird*. Yes, pray to God all you want about me coming back home to you soon to enjoy the lovely sunshine— but my mind's set on one thing only!

I swerve my cab once more through slush and snow, passing men an' women who're still hailing me, flagging me down hard. But, no siree, I won't pick up fellas; and you should see them flailing their arms and cursing me all to high heavens! Another turnaround, then *bam!* I see a tall dude, with no coat on, head shiny bald, like a regular Kojak—he who started this whole damn thing about shaving the hair off your head. What for? Yeah, in some religions it's even a curse to cut off your hair, no?

Oh, the fantasies of some men, walking around only in a dark suit without a coat on when the wind's blowing so hard. This one's now commanding me to stop—and I must pull over, right? Christ, is this black man a director in some large company right here in New York, a fancy executive, so commanding in stature he is? Our people can be truly surprising at times, you betta believe it!

But instinct also tells me this man might be a millionaire by his style and arrogance—and never mind the accursed weather, Harve, I say to myself, think positive now.

I slowly drive to a stop, and he comes over to me; and I must get out and open the door for him in this blizzard. Yeah, I do, and I'm eyeing him all the time, blacker as he is than anyone I've seen around here in quite a while; the snow nevertheless quickly piling on him and covering his face—and what a contrast it will soon be!

He snaps his fingers and glares at me: I must hurry up; and I can tell when a man's in a bad mood. Yeah, maybe I shouldn't have stopped at all. But it's too late now. *Esther, you hear me. Woman, I'm talking to you. Listen to what I'm telling you about this man entering my cab and commanding me to drive him now!*

"Where to?" I ask, deliberately avoiding the word "brother," 'cause this dude's now making me nervous.

He's taking his time to pull off his gloves, a silk-looking ornamented thing, unfit for this weather. And that's another thing about our people who like to dress up—though it might be the only threads they have on, all their worldly possession.

"Where to?" I repeat.

He grimaces.

No, it isn't an illusion that he's in my cab, and I'm looking at him in the rear-view mirror and becoming tense. So I repeat, "Where to?"

"Drive me until I sweat."

"Eh?"

"You heard me!" he barks.

I step on the gas, a sixth sense directing me now; and at once I realize I've made a real mistake in picking him up; and I'm wondering if he's some sort of hood or criminal, or if he's simply gone crazy on this the coldest day of the year. Yeah, weather can make our people go out of their minds, especially in New York.

More anxious I'm becoming, as I sense him looking left and right—and maybe he thinks we're being followed. *By whom?* He closes his eyes, then starts smiling, as I make a quick left turn, then right, to avoid the heavy slush.

Drive me until I sweat. His eyes are now closed, as I look in the mirror once more and grip the steering wheel hard.

I try to create a gyrating motion in the snow, skidding a little here and there. His eyes suddenly open wide, then close, for this man knows what I'm thinking. Oddly, I expect him to start smiling and to say to me, "Hey, brother, I'm just jiving you, man!"

You are?

From the rear-view mirror again, I see he's trying to doze off. Yeah, he's really comfortable-like in my cab with the snow still falling everywhere. Christ, it's my helluva bad luck to pick up such a dude; and odd as it is, as I drive along I begin to think how as a little boy on the island I used to listen to raindrops, drumming on the zinc roof of our small bungalow, and huddling under a blanket I'd be, thinking of one day going to America to make a name for myself!

The dude's eyes quickly open, and I step on the gas once more.

So I say to myself, make sure this man sweats, just as he wants to. I turn on the heat full blast, and drive along 65th Street; and he's reclining comfortably, as if he's the real owner of my *yellah bird.*

Yeah!

It starts to really heat up inside now, and I figure very soon he'll be sweating like a mule . . . and so will I.

He moves his head sideways, jerkily sort of, as if he's stricken with a strange disease. Beads of perspiration start dripping down his long reposeful face, and I expect the same to happen to me too, never mind that I was born in the tropics: and I'm supposed to be used to heat and humidity. I sense him glaring at the back of my head, and again I step on the gas, and all thoughts of making the *holy million* are now gone from my mind. The heat's starting to get to me, though I concentrate on the snow falling outside: on the streets, lawns, parked cars, other vehicles, shops, awnings, everywhere. Suddenly I want to be out there, away from the heat which is becoming stronger. Yeah, before long inside my cab it will become as hot as the equator!

I start testing my senses in a way, anxious to find out if my mind's not playing a trick on me. Perspiration forming on my forehead, and I look in the mirror again; and I see perspiration resting on the bridge of his nose, his nostrils widening. Ah, his eyes close again, and maybe I should tell him he's indeed sweating, just as he wants to do.

Just as I'm about to, he opens his eyes as wide as snookerballs.

Christ!

Once more I concentrate on the wind and snow, skidding a little, yet driving faster, as if on a sudden new impulse.

The next thing I know I'm turning around, going about in a circle more or less, heading back to . . . *No!*

Yeah, I'm now heading in the direction of Staten Island, and it's been almost an hour that I've been driving this dude around, and the *meter* is chalking up the score. And will he pay me? But he seems oblivious of the cost. *Is he really?* At any moment, I expect him to pull out a gun and jab it at the back of my head and holler at me, accuse me of being an immigrant come to America to make things worse for Americans, black as he is an' all!

Esther, d'you hear?

I turn off the meter, thinking I'll put him at ease; and I'm thinking that this fella perhaps isn't a criminal, but someone who wants to work something out of his system, though at my expense. But *why choose me?* I'm praying, telling God that I have a wife back home—the ever-faithful Esther who's always singing allelujahs to herself and to everyone else who will listen. Louder she's singing and praying, and doing the Lord's work; and maybe you're right, Esther; the Big Apple isn't the place to be chasing after the *holy million!*

The dude grimaces, and I want to apologize to him for the inconvenience of this ride. Yeah, should I turn off the heat now, Brother? It's getting to me too, see, tropical-born as I am. Instead, I ask lamely, "How you doin', Mister?"

He grunts.

"I mean, how you doing wid de heat?" I let out a nervous laugh.

The dude's eyelids roll back, as he growls, "Fine. You keep on driving, sucker."

Sucker?

He dabs perspiration from his forehead, then opens and closes his eyes in quick succession, once more. And harder I try to concentrate on the beauty of the snow, as if I have nothing else in the world to think about. Try more positive thinking, see: the lyric beauty of snow everywhere despite the flurries; and the snow's also forming on rooftops in this sky-scraper city, the tall builings everywhere feeling the taste of this blizzard. And I'm thinking again: Man, how can they stand it in places like Canada where it's so close to the North Pole! Esther, she's got a cousin up there, and once she wanted us to go an' live there too. *No, siree!* My eyes meet the dude's instantly.

"You been driving this vehicle long, nigga?" he asks.

"What?" I pretend not to hear him.

"You heard me."

"Three years, na . . . four."

He waits. Then, "That long, huh?"

I want him to keep on talking, cause this way I know what's on his mind. And I hope no gun will suddenly pop out and graze the back my head. Yeah, he's truly sweating now, beads of it rolling down his face; and from time to time he's shaking his head strangely, sort of. Suddenly I want to laugh, as this image grips my mind stronger. *Who's he really?*

Yeah!

But I start thinking about the *holy million* again. Yet I want to tell the dude that this ride's for free, man. Now he better get out of my cab.

Instead I keep quiet, forcing myself to think of the pristine beauty of the snow falling outside.

"Where are we?" he barks.

"Staten Island."

"Again?"

"Yes."

He smiles, and I'm pleased by the friendly tone in his voice now, and for some odd reason I'm also pleased to be taking a black man around, though I know this dude's really taking me for a ride. He leans over my shoulder and peers at the blank meter, and asks how much this ride is costing him. I quickly tell him the meter is turned off, can't he tell?

"What for?" he growls.

I immediately step on the gas again, and maybe I should turn the meter on once more, I'm thinking.

"Take me back to Manhattan," he growls, the sweat coming down his forehead in buckets, hotter as it is.

I quickly roll the window down, but he wants it up at once, and all the time he keeps grunting.

I yearn to have another good look at him in the mirror; and when I do, I note his features, really handsome, bald an' all with a massive forehead. Yes, he's the pride of all that Africa has produced, now right here in my cab in the Big Apple! And, you might never see the likes of him in the Caribbean, I'm also thinking. *But why not?* Esther's voice comes back to me.

He leans forward, as if he knows what's on my mind, and mutters close to my ears: "You got a woman?"

I nod.

"Where's she now?"

"Back home."

"Home?"

"On the island . . . the Caribbean."

He thinks about this for a while, snorts, then laughs; and I can hear him breathing down my neck, and still laughing. Then he points to the snow outside, and I'm not sure what he's thinking now.

I grip the steering wheel hard, controlling the cab as we move up and down.

"What's it like down there, man?"

"Where?" as if I don't know what he's getting at.

"The Caribbean."

"Hot."

He snorts again. "Hot, eh?"

"Yes, really hot."

He's thinking about this for a while, maybe to go there, no? Well, why not? But what will the likes of him do there, where life's so different? And can he survive there? *Can he really? Yeah, he will sweat alright*, I'm telling Esther again.

"What's she doing down there and you's up here?"

135

Is he asking about Esther? I figure I must give this dude a quick answer. "Doing the Lord's work," I say.

He laughs, and just then I nearly steer into the oncoming traffic, with another taxi driver—a Hispanic Jorge or Garcia, whatever his name—suddenly honking at me and threatening to rape my mother!

"Is that true?" The dude seems earnest now, leaning forward a little.

I keep looking straight ahead, as he breathes close to my ears; and he's wet all over, as if he's just come out of a shower. Suddenly I'm thinking about the next letter I will write home to Esther: telling her about this dude for sure, and about some of the types, all God's children, that I meet here in the Big Apple!

Harvey, you're making this up, I hear Esther saying to me.

"It's the Lord's truth, Esther."

You've always been known to make things up.

"It's the truth, woman!"

What's this fellow's name anyway?

Christ, I don't even know, and I glance in the mirror again, and if I ask him now maybe he will tell me!

But immediately I see the dude's face tighten, and he's glaring at me; and Esther's loud laughter comes to me again; and it's this same laughter I miss sometimes living alone here in Brooklyn, when I feel lonely at nights in my small apartment, craving female company. Yes, I continue to hear Esther laughing; while this man's still staring at me . . . from the back.

Yes, tell this dude what I'm really thinking. Tell him too about imagining Esther standing in a corner of Primrose Street back home, a real holy-roller as she is now, shouting the Lord's words: *Hark, ye sinners—beware of Mammon! Beware, for the wages of sin is death, but the gift of God is eternal life!*

Amen!

The dude grunts again close to my ears.

"You okay, Mister?" I ask, feeling the Lord has given me courage to deal with him now. "See, Esther's praying for you . . . and me." Then, quickly, "Well, you're sweating now, no?"

He's wiping off more sweat with his soggy silk hanky, though he's still eyeing me, evilly sort of.

He really is.

When I press on the gas again, I nearly drive straight into the woman at the edge of the sidewalk. I quickly swerve hard again, getting out of the way.

"Hey, take it easy man," the dude yells. I know I've scared him some, and I want to laugh now. And I'm glad to hear the whine in his voice. *Esther, you still with me?*

He keeps looking at me, and I hear the twist of his lips, as if he's now in pain. Maybe he's no longer enjoying the ride.

Swinging ahead again I am, going full speed, even a little recklessly; and Esther's voice, a real barrage of words: *Why don't you come back to the blasted island, Harvey? Why not, eh? You're only living in that God-forsaken place called New Yawk tryin' to make your holy million! But all the time you're picking up pimps an' muggers, and my patience's running out with you, cause I've been waiting long enough for you to make up your mind!*

You see, I have God on my side, and I want you to do the Lord's work standing next to me, right here on this island!

It's as if I'm listening to Esther's voice coming closer and closer, all fire and brimstone as she is now: no longer the quiet, passive woman I once thought she was.

Yeah, imagine me preaching alongside her, really doing the Lord's work right there on Primrose Street, and maybe we'll have our own special congregation—our own followers too; and could this dude become one?

Hey, Brother, do you hear me? Do you see what Esther wants me to do from now on? What d'you say to that, eh? Tell me, man!

A quick glance in the mirror, and a horrified expression comes back to me.

I guess it's the heat doing this to him; and maybe he's goin' a little crazy too, or coming to his senses finally.

I pass a car pulled by a tow truck, then another. Yeah, snow's creating havoc everywhere in the city, and yet I'm going faster, through the blizzard.

"Stop it, man! Stop for God's sake!" the dude yells."You want to kill me! See, I'm sweating already; I really am!"

But I continue to accelerate, as if a strange madness has come over me, cause I'm yet hearing Esther's words about preaching the gospel. And Esther's still complaining: *You see—all the dregs that're now in America: they come from everywhere, landing up in New Yawk City, the same Big Bad Apple of the world, the very one that Eve gave to Adam. Now it's a place of sin an' damnation, you hear! So come back home right now, Harve—I'm pleading with you!*

Her cry is like a clarion shout, all Esther's—believe me—and try as I do I can't escape her.

I press on the gas a little harder.

"Stop it," shouts the dude again, grimacing. "Stop at once!" Then, "It's like the blasted equator in here!"

Suddenly I see him tumbling around in the back seat. "I am as black as you are, see," he pleads. "Let me go, man! You cats from the Caribbean—you're all crazy! Let me go now, p-l-e-a-s-e!"

But I'm not letting him off that easily—after more than an hour he has me driving him around. Yeah, a ride that would've given me over two hundred bucks: helping me to reach the sacred *holy million* that I yearn for!

"You take me for a fool or what?" I rasp, putting on a real island accent now; and it's as if Esther herself is goading me on to it.

I grip the steering wheel harder, my eyes widening, and I'm still looking at the whiteness of snow everywhere, with the wind whipping up. *See, this ain't no jive, Mister. This is the real thing!*

"Let me out, man," he whines.

"I don't hear you," I holler back.

He leans into me, massive forehead an' all, as he dabs perspiration from his neck and face; and all the time he's breathing harder. And Esther's still crying out: *You think America is paradise, eh? Well, paradise is right here on the island—the same one you left five years ago an' think you might never come back to! See, now you don't need no blasted holy million to live with me, Harvey. Here we'll do the Lord's work only, poor as we might be—that'll be all!*

I look in the mirror again, like a bad habit, and I see the twisted expression on his face, mouth contorted, twitching.

"Apologize, man," I say, concentrating on the blank meter and feeling agitated, like a surge of new life injected into my veins.

"What for?" he asks.

I swerve hard, right then left, and the dude lunges sideways, banging his head against the window. I turn swiftly again.

Recovering his balance, he yet tumbles once more, and his voice is one of sharp pain, but which is like sweet music to my ears.

"I APOLOGIZE!"

"That's better."

My eyes are still fixed on the blank meter, and I hear Esther lamenting in her inimitably plaintive voice about a West Indian like me having fallen prey to the *holy million!* Yeah, it's as if I'm suddenly doomed. And she continues talking about the craziness of some people believing in coming to America to make it from rags to riches, black as some of these same people are!

"Please, man, let me outa here," the dude begs. "You're mad as hell, I know."

"Am I?" I ask rhetorically, and smile.

Then I pull over close to a bank of snow, and come to *a dead stop.*

Turning around, I face the dude, eyeballing him, and I sense he's shaking.

He stretches out his hand to the door, and he's still looking at me, with apology on his face. Next he puts his hands into his pocket and starts taking out all the money he has: crumpled dollar bills, more than a hundred, which he's handing to me, one by one, straightening the twisted ends of each note, though I barely look at him.

More snow is falling, and the wind's still picking up, and maybe he's reluctant to leave now. But I stare at him, tall as he is, so really handsome.

Finally he gets out, stepping into a hail wind of snow slapping his face, and he quickly winces. A flurry comes again, as he puts his hands to his eyes to shield himself from the biting cold; and he's about to cry out, suddenly. But all I hear is Esther's voice: *Yeah, Harve, you don't belong with them—these ones who're the real bad apple of America! You belong here close to me on the island!*

I am looking at the dude throwing one dead leg after another, even as he keeps shielding his face from the whiplash of snow. Stumbling, then running forward he is, and suddenly he seems to be in voiceless pain. Then he turns and looks back at me, cause he knows I'm watching him from the safety and shelter of my cab.

I start grinning. And the dollar notes are scattered about on the front seat next to me, all crumpled, looking as if they're all the greenbacks I've been wanting all these years. *Esther, it's already a million, I say!*

The dude's standing about twenty yards away, a forlorn figure in the wilderness of snow, right here in New York City, watching me with a strange beatific smile.

Then slowly he waves, and I instinctively wave back in my island-manner; and again I'm thinking he might be some rich dude, or the executive of a large company here in Manhattan who's just gone off his rocker.

My cab moves slowly forward, as if on its own accord. Again

I press on the gas, and grip the steering wheel—like a bad habit. And I look in the rear-view mirror, and I see my own black face: as if I am the one sitting in the back seat, and I'm still *sweating*, while Esther's laughter comes to me loud and clear—with truly the echo of another place.

140

Acknowledgements

The following stories, edited and revised for this collection, appeared in previous publications: "Mother of Us All" in *India in the Caribbean* edited by David Dabydeen (Hansib, UK, 1988), and *Still Close to the Island* (Commoners Publishing, Canada, 1980); "Los Toros" in *The Dalhousie Review* (Halifax, Canada); "The Pugilist" in *Symbiosis* (Girol Books, Ottawa, 1996); "All For Love" in *Still Close to the Island*; and "Black Jesus" (as "Salvation"), "The Outsider," "Drive Me Until I Sweat" and "Homecoming" in *To Monkey Jungle* (Third Eye Publications, Canada, 1988).